Stevie D

R

Other titles in the series

Stevie Day: Supersleuth
Stevie Day: Lonely Hearts

Stevie Day

Jacqueline Wilson
Rat Race

ARMADA

An Armada Original

First published in the U.K. in 1988 in Armada.

Armada is an imprint of Collins Children's Books
part of the Collins Publishing Group,
8 Grafton Street, London W1X 3LA.

Printed in Great Britain by
William Collins Sons & Co. Ltd., Glasgow

One

I wake up with a start. My Micky Mouse alarm clock is ringing right in my ear. Micky's gloved hands quiver as he points dramatically to the time. He's not solely responsible for the awesome din. The alarm clock is teetering on top of several chipped china plates on an old tin tray, and I've sprinkled teaspoons around to increase the terrible tinkling.

I sit up, smiling. It's quite a clever little invention really. And certainly very effective.

"Stevie!" Carla pokes her head out of the bedclothes, her face screwed up as if she's in some sort of pain. "What's that *noise*?" she groans, and she starts writhing and grimacing. She's a bit of an actress, my sister.

"It's okay. It's just my new alarm system so that I don't sleep in," I say blithely.

"Then switch it off, you great berk!" Carla screams.

She doesn't seem to appreciate my inventiveness. I let Micky ring on a little, rearranging the teaspoons for maximum effect. Carla starts lumbering out of bed, her famous blonde hair in a bit of a tangle. She has murder in her eyes. But she doesn't worry me. She might be as big as me now, but I'm still nearly three years older. And tougher. I can still flatten Carla with one hand tied behind my back. Literally.

As Carla and I are struggling for ascendancy, Micky still ringing fit to bust, Laura starts yelling from her room next door. She's not a very bossy sort of mum, but she's got one particular tone of voice which means Obey Me Instantly. She's using that tone right this minute. I flick the switch and Micky is silent. The teaspoons and plates and tin tray continue to vibrate for a further few seconds before subsiding into silence too.

"Is it a fire, Laura?" six-year-old Poppy calls, and we hear her running into Laura's room.

"No. Just Stevie. Sending us all stark raving mad as usual," Laura says loudly.

"I just wanted to make sure we didn't all sleep in," I call to her, injured.

"I don't think there's any fear of that now," says Laura.

We hear her bedsprings creak as Poppy climbs in for a cuddle. Carla huddles under her bedclothes again, mumbling obscenities at me. What a surly, sleepy family. Apart from me. I give Micky a little nod of thanks and bounce out of bed.

It's now nearly five minutes past seven on Monday morning. Don't get me wrong. I don't normally bounce out of bed. Not this early. And especially not on a Monday.

I usually lurk as long as I can, thinking about the homework that I've somehow failed to do over the weekend. And Double Maths (if you only understand 0.5% in a 40 minute session what is the percentage of your understanding if said session is doubled??). And I might be wondering if I can hop through an entire Hockey lesson because I hurled my boots at a crowd of stupid boys and one of them (boots, not boys) somehow spiralled up and up through the air and onto the school roof and stayed there. *You* know those depressing early Monday morning thoughts.

But there's no feeling of gloom and doom *this* particular Monday. Because there's no school. Well, no lessons. Some of my form are off on this wonderful five day trip to Paris. Including me!

I wasn't sure I was going to get to go for ages. I knew there wasn't much point asking Laura. She'd fork out for us all to have a holiday if she could, but she simply doesn't have the money. She has this stall at the Antique Emporium but she doesn't really make that much out of it. I've got a Saturday newspaper round but that's not exactly highly profitable either.

So I asked Dad. I didn't want to ask him, but I could see he was my only hope. I don't really get on that well with my Dad. Not since he walked out on us and went to live with the lady friend Marianne who is now his wife. But he's rich and he'll spend extra money on Carla and Poppy and me if he thinks it's for sound educational purposes.

So I stressed the absolutely incredible educational purpose of our school trip to Paris. I told him about all these museums and art galleries on the itinerary and elaborated on the opportunities for me to air my French and communicate with the natives. And so he agreed and paid up and now today I'm off to Paris, hurray hurray. Or *Hourra Hourra*, as the French say. Not that I'm going to bother to try to yatter away in a fancy foreign lingo. Or trail round boring old museums. Who wants to study on holiday? I'm off to enjoy myself.

That doesn't mean I won't work hard too. I shall have my eyes peeled. They don't call me Stevie Day Supersleuth for nothing. You never know my luck. I might just stumble upon some Mr Big – sorry, Monsieur Grand – in Paris and end up with the whole of Interpol fawning at my feet. I might still be at school but I've solved several serious cases already and I'm best friends with the famous detective Cathy Cope. Well, she's not exactly a detective yet, but she's working plain clothes in our local Crime Squad and she's obviously going to be made a detective any minute.

Cathy lent me her weekend bag to take on my Paris trip. (We've just got one huge battered family suitcase and a selection of plastic carriers.) I'm thrilled with Cathy's bag. It's one of these stylish squashy black leather numbers with lots of zips and secret pockets. Great for a detective. I asked her if she'd used the bag on any exciting cases. You could hide a gun in one pocket, mini-binoculars in another, camera and tape recorder in the main partition . . . Cathy laughed and said I'd been watching too many old James Bond movies.

I squat on my bedroom floor and check all the secret pockets now. No guns or flashy equipment, needless to say. But my passport and my purse are still pretty exciting all the same. I've never had a passport before. The farthest I've ever been is the Isle of Wight, which is hardly an exotic foreign clime.

I flip through my passport, wincing a little at the photograph. It seemed a good idea to pull a funny face in the photo booth but now it's not quite so amusing. And the description of me on the opposite page is a bit disappointing too.

Laura wouldn't let me fill in the form properly. I still don't see why I can't claim "detective" as an occupation when I've been busy this past year detecting things left right and centre. And she wouldn't even let me put anything in the Distinguishing Marks box. I have got some terribly distinguished marks. I've a good mind to ink in one or two right this minute. No. Better not.

I go through my purse instead. The contents seem very sparse. Just three little pieces of paper. These 100 franc notes don't look like real money at all. It doesn't look as if I've got my thirty odd pounds worth. Still, even though it doesn't look much it certainly sounds a fortune. Three hundred francs spending money! I've never had so much in all my life. And oh boy – oh garçon

8

– I'm going to spend and spend and spend.

"You promise you'll bring me back something really stylish from Paris?" Carla says sleepily, still under the bedclothes. "Earrings. Or a teeshirt with a French motif. Well, I'd like a bag even better, but I don't suppose – "

"You don't suppose correctly, Carla," I say crisply.

Yes, holiday presents are going to burn a bit of a hole in my funds. There's Poppy too. And Laura. And I want to give Cathy something nice, as she's lending me her bag. And then there's Dad. I don't want to give him anything but I suppose he did cough up the money for the trip. I sigh.

"I don't know what you're sighing for, you lucky beast," says Carla. "I'd give anything to go to Paris. It's not fair. Why is it just you older ones who get to go?"

"Because we're mature enough to appreciate a sophisticated city like Paris, my petal," I say smugly.

The fourth and fifth years aren't acting very maturely when we roll up outside the school an hour later. They're all pushing and shoving to get on the coach first, yelling and screaming and bobbing about, while Mrs Wainwright and Mr Mason and Ms Mosely rush about like anxious sheepdogs, trying to round everyone up.

It's not fair. We've all been told we've got to travel in boring babyish school uniform but all three teachers are in their holiday gear. Mrs Wainwright is actually in *trousers* – and with her backside too! Mr Mason is all laid back and lovely in a white teeshirt and a tight pair of 501s. No wonder all the girls are goggle-eyed. But he only has eyes for Ms Mosely.

I can't stick Ms Mosely. It's bad enough saying her name. When we all say good morning to her at the start of each art session we sound like a great swarm of bees. She always says she's a great believer in free expression but whenever I express myself freely she gets really angry. And she's meant to be this committed feminist

9

and yet whenever there's a man around she tosses her curls and flutters her eyelashes. Look at her now in her tiny little teeshirt dress, toss toss, flutter flutter, while Mr Mason stares transfixed.

"Hey, Stevie!

It's my friend Terry, his head right out of the coach window.

"Come on, Stevie. Me and my mates have bagged the back seat," he yells. "Come and sit with us."

All Terry's mates howl and scream and pull hideous faces in accompaniment.

I glance over my shoulder at a certain girl in our form called Lucy. She used to hang round my friend Terry. She sometimes seems to kid herself that he fancies her. She's having a little pout right this minute. I smile. I wave cheerily at Terry. But I don't really want to sit with him and all his Neanderthal companions, thanks very much.

"I'm sitting with Hazel, Terry," I call.

There's Hazel now, panting along the road, with her Mum on one side and her Nan on the other. What's she got in her hand?

"Stevie, Stevie! Look! See my camera? Nan won it at the Bingo just last night. Isn't it great? Want me to take your picture? You and your Mum and your sisters."

Yes, they're all here to see me off. Carla looks envious. Poppy looks bored. And Laura looks worried.

"You will behave yourself, won't you, Stevie?" she keeps saying. "You won't muck about too much? You won't play around on the boat? You won't wander off by yourself in Paris? You won't do anything silly and get into trouble?"

"Don't you trust me, Laura?" I say, wounded.

"Not an inch," says Laura, but then she gives me a sudden hug.

I hug her back, although I feel a prize banana in front

of all my friends.

"Look after yourself and have a lovely time," says Laura.

Hazel snaps away with her camera, recording our emotional farewell for all posterity – along with Carla's cross face and Poppy in the middle of picking her nose.

Then Hazel photographs her Mum and Nan and then starts prancing about trying to get the whole coach into focus.

"Take it easy, Hazel. You won't have any film left for when we get to Paris," I say.

"Come along, you girls, you'd better get on the coach," says Mrs Wainwright. She sounds a little sour. Mr Wainwright has come to see her off, but he's standing in a corner now with Ms Mosely, utterly engrossed.

I give Laura one more hug, waggle my tongue at Carla, tickle Poppy under the chin – and then spring up the steps into the coach. I wander up and down the aisle, trying to choose the best seat. Some stupid boys won't get out of the way – and Lucy's flouncing around at my back, demanding to get past.

"Will you sit down this minute, Stephanie Day!" Mrs Wainwright calls. "You're blocking everybody's way."

Me! But I can sense it's not the right time to start arguing. So I sit down and give Laura and co. one last wave through the window. Hazel sits beside me, tucking her new camera into its case as tenderly as if it were a baby. Our friend Michelle is sitting across the aisle from us – next to Elaine. I don't know why she's pulled up with *her*. Elaine is a Pain. She's got scraped-back hair and little round glasses and a high-pitched voice and if she was in a comic strip there would be a big arrow with SCHOOL SWOT pointing straight at her. She's the swottiest swot ever. And true to form she's now clutching this boring guide book to Paris.

When the coach gets going she starts spouting out all these facts and figures which drive me absolutely dotty. I mean, does it really *matter* how many rivets there are in the Eiffel Tower? (Two and a half million if you really want to know.)

"How would you fancy a rivet up your nose, Elaine?" I suggest.

She takes no notice, droning on and on like an intellectual mosquito. Just *occasionally* she happens on a piece of slightly more interesting information – like the fact you can sometimes see for forty two miles from the top of the Tower.

"I'm dying to go up it, aren't you, Hazel?" I say. "Think of the pictures you'll be able to take with your camera. Here, I bet it shakes like anything in the wind."

Hazel is looking a little odd. She's a strange pale green and her eyes are closed.

"Are you feeling sick? I hope you're not going to vomit copiously all over my school blazer? Because it's not mine. I had to borrow it from Carla because Laura said my own blazer's too much of a disgrace. Just because of that chewing gum on the sleeve. And the ink. And the oil marks up the back. Hazel?"

"I'm not feeling sick," Hazel mutters. "My Nan gave me a travel sickness pill."

"Well, you look as if you could do with a few more. If you're like this on the coach what are you going to be like on the boat? When the waves go up and down, *up* and *down* – "

"Shut up, Stevie."

"Sorry, sorry."

Elaine's voice drones ever onwards. She's finished the Eiffel Tower now and started on the surrounding district. She mutters on about museums and I take no notice, but then she suddenly mentions sewers.

"*Sewers*?" I say.

"Yes. Egouts. That's French for sewers," says Elaine.

"You can go round real sewers? Your actual sewers with a mauvais pong and beaucoup de grands rats? *That's* French for – "

"I know," says Elaine sharply.

"I want to go and see these sewers! Haze, you'll come with me, won't you? Wow! Just think of all those égout-rats scrabbling around in the dark." I turn my hands into scrabbly sewer rats and tickle Hazel. "What's French for squeak?"

"Taisez-vous," says Hazel, trying to squirm free. "That's French for shut *up*."

"Stephanie Day, whatever are you doing now?" Mrs Wainwright calls down the coach.

It's not fair. She's obviously going to keep picking on me all holiday.

Terry and his mates have started a sing-song at the back of the coach. Quite softly at first, because they're rather rude songs. But then they get louder and louder. Mr Mason tells them to put a sock in it, and suggests they try something French if they really must sing.

They bellow *Frère Jacques* a few times and then run out of steam. I start up a feminist version about *Soeur Jacqueline* but it's not really that catchy. So I try adapting a few well-known English songs into French.

We sing *La chanson des oiseaux* with all the appropriate gestures. Then we launch into *Tie a ruban jaune around le vieux oak arbre*. Then *Combien est le chien dans la fenêtre*? Then all ten verses of *Dix bouteilles vertes*. And as we approach Dover at last then naturally we sing *There'll be oiseaux bleus over les blancs cliffs de Dover*.

There's a great kerfuffle getting us all off the coach, through Customs and onto the boat. We have to stand

13

in a queue for ages, crowded up with all these other travellers. There's a lot of other schools on trips. Mrs Wainwright growls at us, because our party is by far the noisiest. There's a lot of students too, mostly lumbering about with enormous backpacks.

"How can they bear all that weight?" says Hazel, who's finding her own small suitcase enough of a struggle. "If I tried to wear one of those rucksacks I'd just keel right over."

I stare at one particularly weird student with little twitchy eyes, sweat on his brow – and a rucksack the size of a small house. He's even got odd bits and bundles tied on the outside, dangling precariously.

"Look at that one! Here, what about if I try barging into him to see if he topples?"

"*No*, Stevie!" says Hazel. She's never sure when I'm joking. I'm not always sure either, come to think of it.

The sweaty student with the outsize rucksack finds it really hard work lumbering up the steep gangplank onto the boat. He wobbles alarmingly, at a very odd angle.

"Don't get too near him. We don't want to get squashed flat," I say.

All his little dangling parcels sway in the breeze – and as he makes the last desperate lurch onto the boat one of them gets caught. He lumbers forward, oblivious, and the string snaps.

I dart forward and pick up the fallen parcel. It's a small brown paper package. There's something quite soft inside. Soft – and sort of squashy. I prod at it carefully. It's not just one thing. There are several separate things, but they're joined together in some way. Four things. I feel again to make sure. They feel just like four big fat fingers.

I hold the package at arm's length, my heart thudding.

14

"Hazel," I whisper. "Here Hazel, have a feel of this."

But the student has turned. He's looking at me. He sees me holding the package.

"Oh! Did it drop off? Thanks very much," he says, and he snatches it out of my hand.

He lumbers off – and I grab Hazel excitedly.

"Come on! I've got to keep an eye on him. I'm sure he's got something incredibly disgusting in that package. You'll never guess."

"So tell me," says Hazel. "And we can't go off and follow him, Stevie. We've all got to keep together, Mrs Wainwright said."

"Promise you won't laugh at me?" I lean close to her ear and whisper.

"You what?" says Hazel. "I can't hear, you're just tickling my ear. Come *on*, Stevie, let's go after the others."

"A severed hand!" I hiss dramatically.

Hazel hears this time. She also laughs, a little nervously.

"I said *don't* laugh."

"Well, stop messing about."

"I'm not. I felt the *fingers*, Hazel."

"Will you just shut up, Stevie," says Hazel, shuddering.

"Stephanie Day, will you come over here this minute! And you too, Hazel. We're all waiting for you," Mrs Wainwright bellows, approaching rapidly.

If I can't convince Hazel I know there's no chance with Mrs Wainwright. So I have to join up with all the others and listen to this boring old lecture about Behaving Ourselves and Not Running Wild and Children aren't allowed Duty Free Fags and Boats can be Dangerous Places. You know the usual stuff. But eventually she runs out of steam and says we can go off

15

and explore for a bit and have our packed lunches.

Hazel wants to repack her lunch into her stomach straight away but for once food is not my major concern.

"I want to find that student with the big rucksack," I say determinedly.

"Stevie!" Hazel moans, but she knows it's no use arguing with me when my mind's made up.

We trail up and down our deck, but he's not in the café or at the bar or in any of the seats. He could be in the Gents, of course, but I don't think it likely. I hang around outside each Gents for several minutes to make sure.

"People are looking at us, Stevie," Hazel says, very red in the face. "You're mad. You were just imagining things. Can't we have our lunch now? And then I want to go up on the top deck to take some photos of the sea."

"Maybe that's where he's gone," I say. "Let's look up there now."

And he *is* up on the outside deck, although it's so wild and windy now we're out at sea that he has to cling hard to the railings to keep his footing. He stops and unloads his huge rucksack, and it thuds onto the deck.

"What's he *got* in there?" I hiss into Hazel's ear. "It's so heavy. "A real dead weight. Oh Hazel. A *dead weight*! Maybe that's what it is! Maybe he's got a whole body in there."

"Don't be ridiculous," says Hazel. Hunger has got the better of her, and she's hurriedly munching marmite sandwiches.

"He's got the butchered body inside the rucksack – or a grisly torso at the very least. Maybe that big round parcel hanging outside is the head!"

"Rubbish," says Hazel, but she's not chewing so vigorously.

"And all the other parcels could be chopped up bits of body," I continue relentlessly. "And do you know what I think he's doing, Haze? He's going to chuck them all in the sea when he thinks no one's looking. Yes, he's committed some foul and terrible murder and now he's very cleverly getting rid of the body. He hasn't left it in one lump in case someone sees it and fishes it out. No, he's chopped it up into manageable pieces and he's going to scatter it all over the English Channel."

"You talk the most terrible garbage, Stevie. I know perfectly well you're just kidding, trying to work me up into a state," says Hazel.

Is she right? Maybe. And yet . . .

"Look!" I shriek, and I point with a shaking finger.

There's something red and sticky slowly seeping out of one of his packages onto the deck. Blood!

Two

"See!" I hiss. "Look at it. Drip drip drip – "

"Don't," says Hazel, shuddering.

"I knew it, I just *knew* it. So what bit's in the dripping package? A foot?"

"Will you just shut *up*, Stevie," says Hazel. She tries to swallow and chokes on her marmite sandwich.

I pat her smartly on the back, trying to gather my thoughts. I wonder about going to Mrs Wainwright now – but she's still going to need an awful lot of convincing.

"Proof," I say. "That's what we need. Evidence."

"What?" Hazel gasps between coughs.

"Hazel, would you mind choking to death on some other occasion? We're too busy at this particular moment. We've got to get evidence. Then we'll make people believe us."

"What do you mean, evidence?" says Hazel, still obstinately coughing.

I sigh. "You can't genuinely be this thick – you're just doing it to annoy me. We've got to get some sort of evidence that proves old sweaty twitcher over there is a mad butcher with a rucksack full of human joints."

"I could take a photo of him with my new camera!" Hazel says, beaming with pride at this sudden inspiration. "There, Stevie. That would be evidence."

"No it wouldn't. It'd just be a photo of a weird looking bloke with a big rucksack. It wouldn't prove a thing."

"You'd be able to see the blood."

"You'd just see this little blurry bit of red, that's all. No. What I need is *real* evidence. One of those little packets. Just think, I had the fingers in my own hand. If only I'd hung on to them instead of handing them straight back like a fool. I could kick myself." I kick at my own ankles savagely. It doesn't help, it just dirties my socks.

"Whatever are you doing?" asks Hazel.

"Teaching myself a lesson," I say, wincing. "I'm going to try to grab one of his parcels, Hazel. The bloody one. I've got to make sure it's real evidence, and not just his clean underpants or whatever."

"You can't! You can't hold it, not if it's got a – a *foot* inside." Hazel gives an enormous shudder.

I'm not too thrilled at the idea myself, but it seems to be the only way. And I'd better get a move on, before he starts scattering all his gruesome parcels into the Channel. So how am I going to go about it? I could just stroll up, grab at a parcel, and run. But what if he runs after me? I'm very speedy on my feet, but without his rucksack he might be able to run fast too. And he's not the sort of bloke it's safe to mess around with. Particularly if he realizes I'm on to him. He must be quite strong or he could never cope with that huge rucksack. All it would take is one lunge, one grab, and then I'd be over the railings and splash into the sea. I might be a good swimmer but I'm not quite ready to have a crack at crossing the Channel.

"How can I get that package without him noticing?" I say, pondering determinedly.

"You can't," says Hazel, who's always been a bit of a defeatist.

"Oh come on, Haze, help me. I know! You can create a diversion."

"No," says Hazel immediately.

"Oh go on, it's the only way. You won't have to do

anything too complicated. You could just . . . faint?"

"*No*," says Hazel. "What do you think I am, Stevie? I can't faint anyway."

"I'm not asking you to faint properly. Just pretend. Think about all the bloody bits of toe and finger, that will help things on a bit, make you look genuinely pale."

"I'm not fainting. It would mean falling on the floor and I'd end up breaking my leg or something, and anyway I've just had my school uniform cleaned for the holiday."

"You could just pretend to go a bit dizzy. Or – or choke! That's it. Get your sandwiches out again. Chomp away, and we'll go and stand right beside him, and then you can start coughing just the way you did before and I'll get him to help you – and then while he's administering first aid I'll find a way of nicking one of his parcels."

"If he's a murderer then why would he bother helping me?" says Hazel. "What if he tries to butcher me too? Oh Stevie, let's go back and find the others. Can't we forget all about him?"

"We can't possibly turn our backs on a murderer! What if he goes on butchering helpless women? It would be partly our fault because we didn't try to stop him. Don't worry, we're not going to try anything stupid. As soon as I get hold of the parcel we'll take it straight to Mrs Wainwright or – or the captain of the ship – anyone, it doesn't matter. And they can deal with it. And him. And he'll be caught and it'll all be down to us. Well, me, actually. I was the one who spotted him and put two and two together."

"Then you go and get his parcel all by yourself," says Hazel grumpily.

"All right," I say, just to show her, and I start staggering along the heaving deck towards him. I go right up to the railings, gasping a little as the wind and spray slap at my face. I look sideways as casually as I can. He's staring

20

at me, looking a little wary. I'm feeling more than a little wary myself. But I can't really chicken out now. I edge a bit closer to him. Then closer still.

He's still looking at me. I suppose it does seem a bit odd. We've practically got the deck to ourselves and yet here am I sidling up to him until we're virtually cheek to cheek.

How am I going to grab the bloody parcel? Just reach down and then make a run for it? I grip the railing tightly to stop my hands trembling. I stare out to sea for inspiration. I've got to do something soon or it'll be too late. I think that faint blur in the far distance is Calais.

I pull myself together, about to snatch and scarper, when I hear a violent coughing noise. I whip round – and the student does too. There's wonderful old Hazel staggering up to us, half-eaten sandwich waving in the air. She coughs, she splutters, she chokes. I couldn't put on a better performance myself. She even does little snorty wheezes as if she can't quite catch her breath.

"Help! My friend! She's choking," I cry. "Can you give her a big pat on the back, quick!"

The student looks sweatier than ever, his eyes going twitch twitch twitch – but he approaches Hazel gingerly and taps her back half-heartedly. And I bend down swiftly, snap the bloody parcel from its string, and stick it inside my blazer. Done!

Then I go up to them, putting my arm round Hazel.

"Thanks ever so much," I say to the student. "There, your pat seems to have done the trick. Honestly, she's awful, she's always choking like that. She doesn't chew her food properly. Well, she can't, she's got these funny false teeth, you see, it's a shame. I'll take her downstairs now and get her a drink of water. Thanks again."

I steer Hazel round the corner.

"I *haven't* got false teeth!" Hazel hisses indignantly. "What did you have to tell him that for?"

"Well, I had to say something, just to try and make it sound convincing."

"I haven't even got any *fillings*, let alone false teeth. Nan always makes me brush my teeth three times a – "

"Will you shut up about your boring teeth, Hazel. They're hardly the point."

"Well, I thought the whole point was you grabbing that parcel, only you messed it up, didn't you?"

"Of course I didn't!"

"Well where is it?"

I open my blazer proudly.

"Stevie! Yuck! Ugh! The blood! It's all over your sweater – and look at the inside of your blazer."

I remember too late that it's not actually my blazer. Carla isn't going to be very pleased with me. It's horrible blood. Very red and thick. Congealed. I decide to hold the package at arm's length. There's something long and hard inside.

"It can't be a foot, it's not the right shape," I say. "It feels more like a piece of arm or leg."

Hazel makes about-to-be-sick noises.

"Put it *down*, Stevie, it's still dripping," she says, shuddering.

But I've got to hang on to it at all costs. I finger the edge of the paper and the remains of the string.

"We ought to look inside – just to make sure," I say.

Hazel's noises increase in intensity. She cowers away from the parcel as if the severed arm – or leg – might attack her. Then she breathes a sudden sigh of relief.

"Oh Stevie, look over there, by the steps. It's Mr Mason and Ms Mosely!"

"So it is!" I look at them with interest. Ms Mosely is staggering about although the deck isn't heaving *that* much. Mr Mason takes her arm to steady her. He keeps hold of her arm. She looks up at him, her curls blowing in the wind. Talk about quick work! They haven't even got to Paris yet.

But there's no time to speculate on their potential holiday romance – not now, anyway. I dash across the deck, holding the bloody parcel, Hazel panting along behind me.

"Ms Mosely! Mr Mason!"

They freeze – and then jump apart. They both look very annoyed indeed.

"What are you doing up here, Stevie? And you, Hazel? Why aren't you downstairs having lunch with all the others?" says Mr Mason.

"Mrs Wainwright said we could explore. And we did. And there's this student, he's over there, the one with the backpack – and you'll never guess what he's got inside it!"

"Astonish us then, Stevie," says Ms Mosely in a very unsisterly tone.

"Bits of body," I say dramatically.

They don't react in the way I expect. They just seem *irritated*.

"I know you and Hazel might think this little joke hysterically funny, Stevie, but –"

"It's no joke! Look! I grabbed one of his packages. There! See the blood." I wave it in their faces.

Mr Mason takes hold of the parcel. He looks at it carefully. He puts it right up to his face, smelling it. And then – oh I can't *believe* it – he *licks* it.

Hazel and I shudder violently. Even Ms Mosely looks considerably disconcerted. She's found out in the nick of time that her intended lover goes in for Vampiric Perversions.

"Tomato sauce," says Mr Mason, seeing our faces. He peels off the soggy paper and exposes an HP tomato sauce bottle, cracked at the bottom so that it's leaking all over the place.

"Tomato sauce," I repeat slowly, feeling sick.

23

"Hey! You girls!" It's the twitchy student, sweating across the deck towards us, rucksack abandoned. "What are you up to, eh? You! The short-haired one. You took my tomato sauce. What are you playing at? First it was my sausages as I was getting on the boat – and now my tomato sauce. And you've *broken* it!"

"I didn't break it, honestly. It was cracked already. I saw the red dripping out of the parcel. That's why I took it. Because – because I thought it might be a severed arm. Or leg. Whatever," I say, and even I can see it does sound a bit foolish now. "I felt the sausages and I thought they were fingers and so . . ."

"But why did you think I was going round with all these bits of body?" says the student, sounding baffled.

"Well – I sort of thought you might be a murderer," I say.

"Stevie!" says Mr Mason.

"Stevie!" says Ms Mosely.

The student says nothing for a moment. He looks twitchier than ever. Oh no, I think I've really hurt his feelings. He's actually shaking. And then he snorts. And roars with laughter.

"Me, a murderer?" he splutters.

"I thought you had the torso in your rucksack and that's why it was so heavy," I say, starting to giggle myself.

"I've got all my camping gear stashed inside. There wasn't room for my food, so I tied it on in little parcels. And you thought . . ." He's hooting with laughter again.

I'm so glad he's got a sense of humour. But Mr Mason and Ms Mosely don't seem to be finding it so funny. They make me apologize profusely, despite the fact he really doesn't seem to mind now. Hazel has to join in the humble apologies, even though I nobly insist on taking the blame. Then Mr Mason sends us down to the lower deck with various Awful Warnings about Last Chances to Behave – Or Else.

"Do you think they'll tell Mrs Wainwright?" says Hazel worriedly. "She'll absolutely do her nut."

"Of course they won't tell," I say. "They obviously sneaked up to the top deck to be by themselves. They left Mrs Wainwright to cope with all us lot, which was a bit of a mean trick in itself. So of course they're not going to tell tales on us, or they'll have to come clean about their little upper deck love tryst."

"Their what?" says Hazel, giggling.

"I think we're going to have to keep a weather eye on those two this holiday," I say. "We can't have them cavorting around X-certificate style, corrupting our innocent young minds."

"I wouldn't mind a cavort with Mr Mason," says Hazel, sighing. "Oh Stevie, didn't he look *fabulous* when he was telling you off? So *stern*."

"Would you mind putting a chausette in it, Hazel?" I say.

"Stephanie Day? And you Hazel! Where have you two *been*? Come over here at once!"

It's the familiar Wainwright-wail, and Hazel and I hasten to obey.

We're all given another long lecture about Getting Off the Boat and Onto the Train. You'd think we were all in Class One of the Infants.

I can't wait to get my foot on foreign soil – even though French quayside concrete doesn't seem that different from English. I rather fancy prostrating myself like the Pope and giving it a kiss, but the Wainwright glower is right behind me and I can sense it would not be wise.

The twitchy student lumbers past Hazel and me as we walk through the custom hall and he suddenly contorts his face into a mad murdering leer and makes wild strangling gestures with his hands. Hazel and I hoot with

25

laughter, but Mrs Wainwright comes rushing up protect-
ively and bustles us out of his way.

"Take no notice, girls. He's probably harmless," she
says hurriedly, and she gets irritated when we laugh even
louder.

The train journey to Paris is a bit of a bore. The
countryside doesn't look *French* enough somehow. I
don't spot a single bloke in a black beret, and all the
women look boringly ordinary, not a bit French Fashion
Plate. The French people that get on the train at Amiens
don't even whiff of garlic. It's all a great disappointment.

I perk up when we get to Paris though. The Gare du
Nord is this great bustling lively place – and it's all a bit
too great and bustling and lively for Mrs Wainwright and
Mr Mason and Ms Mosely, because they're not sure
which Metro we have to take to get to our hotel, and
when Mrs Wainwright asks someone in her best School-
mistressy French they just wave her out of their way dis-
dainfully. Mr Mason consults his metro map but before
he can work it out Ms Mosely has sidled up to this really
stylish smouldering Frenchman and fluttered her
eyelashes helplessly.

"Ah yes, Mademoiselle. I zinc I can 'elp you," he says,
exactly like someone out of *'Allo 'Allo*.

He helps us all on and off the right metros, and when
we emerge successfully at the Arc de Triomphe we all
give him a grateful wave while he insists it has been his
pleasure, he is only too 'appy to 'elp.

"The Arc de Triomphe commemorates Napoleon's
victories," says Elaine. "And there are twelve avenues
leading off from it. The Champs-Elysées must be over
there. It's the most famous avenue in Paris, and it's got
lots of expensive cafés and luxurious shops."

"And is that where we're staying?" I say. "Gosh,
gracious living at last!"

I picture our hotel, an elegant mansion with flower

26

strewn balconies. I imagine each bedroom: cream silk bedcover, cream velvet chaise longue, fluffy cream carpet . . . the ultimate in French style, French chic, French luxury.

Our hotel isn't on the Champs-Elysées. It's up another avenue, along a couple of streets, down a narrow road crammed with market stalls and round another corner. Our hotel isn't at all stylish, chic or luxurious. But it *is* French. And I suppose that's all that matters.

There's a most formidable Madame who stalks around with a boot face, giving *Mrs Wainwright* a little lecture about Standards and Behaviour and Unruly Enfants. Mrs Wainwright gets very red in the face and when Madame eventually marches off, high heels clicking like jackboots, Mrs Wainwright passes the lecture on to us. Mr Mason and Ms Mosely are standing in a corner by themselves, having a private whisper. Mrs Wainwright starts allocating bedrooms and handing out keys. I wouldn't mind betting Mr Mason and Ms Mosely are hoping for a shared bedroom – but no, Mr Mason gets a single right up in the roof, whereas Ms Mosely is on the second floor at the other end of the building. We'll have to watch out for a lot of complicated corridor wandering!

Hazel hopes for a top floor attic for us, so she can go to sleep fantasizing about Mr Mason just the other side of her bedroom wall – but no such luck, we get the first floor too, right next to Mrs Wainwright!

"So I can keep an eye on you," she says grimly.

Hm! And Haze and I have got to share too, with Michelle and Elaine. Michelle's okay, but Elaine! I can't stand the thought of her droning on and on all holiday. My head can only absorb a certain number of deeply boring facts before it reaches bursting point and explodes.

It's a very little room. Madame has crammed in two smallish double beds, one wardrobe, and one tiny table

27

and chair – and that's your lot. There's no room for us too. You can't walk across the room, you have to hop onto the bed and bounce for it.

"I think it's more roomy in the bathroom," I say, going to investigate.

There isn't a *bath*, of course. Nor a loo. We know all about bidets, thank you very much. Although I'm still not quite clear how you . . . And I don't fancy experimenting to find out, not in full view of Hazel, Michelle and the Pain. There's a perfectly conventional basin – though when I give my hands a much-needed wash the plumbing gives several immensely vulgar explosive gurgles which make us all collapse with the giggles.

"Now then, girls, why are you all being so silly?" says Mrs Wainwright, bursting in on us.

Teachers have got a cheek. They'd be furious if we tried bursting into *their* bedrooms.

Mrs Wainwright tells us to get a move on, because Madame will be serving up our evening meal in ten minutes and we haven't even started unpacking yet.

"Can we change into our proper clothes, Mrs Wainwright?" asks Hazel.

Mrs Wainwright can't really say no – and it's very interesting when we all gather downstairs in the dining room. Hazel and I don't look so very different. I'm just in my jeans, and Haze is in her dungarees. Michelle still has to wear quite babyish clothes and Elaine doesn't look very startling in her pinafore dress – but some of the girls have really gone to town. Thick make-up, very high heels, tiny little tight skirts.

"Look at Lucy," says Hazel, sighing.

She's in a white skirt to match her white heels, and she's got this pink angora sweater that makes her look cuter and cuddlier than ever. She somehow manages to sit next to Terry at the table. He's very red in the face but he doesn't seem to mind. Until her angora starts

28

shedding and he starts sneezing.

"Oh dear. Lucy's getting right up his nose," I say, grinning.

I'm too interested in sampling genuine French Cuisine to pay much attention to boring little Lucy of course. I hope for something ultra exotic like snails. I'm out of luck. We start off with watery legume soup. That's your common or garden vegetable, and a carrot is a carrot, no matter which country you're in. The main course is frankfurters and frites. Sausage and chips aren't exactly foreign either. And it's just two smallish frankfurters and not a lot of frites. I hope for an enormous pudding – one of those wonderful French fruit tarts, perhaps. No. It's a carton of yoghurt. It's French. But that's about it.

I'm still starving afterwards. Mrs Wainwright reluctantly agrees to our going off for a little explore, so long as we stick together in groups of four or more.

There's a little café at the corner of our street.

"Let's go and have an ice-cream or something," I say. "What's ice-cream in French, eh?"

"It's glace," says Elaine. "So if you want a strawberry ice-cream it's glace à la fraise."

Occasionally I can see some slight point in going round with Elaine. We go into the café and sit down at a table in a corner, beside a smart middle-aged man and a girl about twenty. He's a bit like my Dad actually. He frowns at us lot and shunts up a bit, away from us. *Very* like my Dad.

An amazingly French waiter comes zooming up, natty little moustache and maroon waistcoat, a silver tray balanced in one hand. He says something in remarkably rapid French, so quick that even Elaine doesn't catch what he's saying. Nevertheless, she tries to start asking for four strawberry ices.

The waiter interrupts curtly. "Je ne comprends pas," he snaps.

29

Poor Elaine goes scarlet, and has another go, her voice shaking a bit.

It still doesn't get us anywhere. The man who looks like my Dad is English. I hear him muttering about silly little schoolgirls. "You couldn't order for us, could you?" I ask. "We want four strawberry ices."

He sighs, beckons to the waiter and gabbles out a stream of French that actually *sounds* French. And the waiter understands and trots off.

"Thanks ever so much," I say. "You speak really good French. Do you live over here, or are you just on a holiday like us?"

But he doesn't seem to want to be drawn into conversation. He just shakes his head, and then practically turns his back on us. He talks to the girl in a low voice. She whispers back. I think they're holding hands under the table.

Our strawberry ices arrive, in dear little silver bowls, but Stevie Day Supersleuth cannot be diverted. My ears flap. I distinctly hear the girl whisper "I can't help feeling so scared."

Aha! I know why!

Three

That man's even more like my Dad than I thought. I know exactly why that girl is feeling so scared. She's scared his *wife* will find out about them.

I stare at them disapprovingly. It's so obvious. He's much older than she is. Much richer and classier too. He's a real Mr Smoothie. Maybe he's her boss. He's certainly in charge.

She looks uneasy and nervous. She keeps looking round anxiously, nibbling the skin on her lip, fiddling with her hair. I expect she's terrified someone will spot them and put two and two together.

It's obvious why she's got herself involved with him. She keeps looking up at him in this quivery Bambi way, all adoring big eyes. He's talking to her a great deal. She just gives little nods and mumbles, happy to let him lay down the law.

I've seen my Dad going on like that to Marianne. It makes me feel sick.

"Stevie?" Hazel gives me a nudge. "Stevie, why are you glaring at that couple like that?"

"Because I think they're awful."

"Why? He was nice, he helped us get our ice-cream. Don't you like yours? You've hardly touched it."

"Give us a chance," I say, starting to wolf it down.

Mr Smoothie's putting his arm round the girl now, try-ing to calm her down.

"Ah. Don't they look romantic," says Hazel.

"Yuck! You call that romantic? He's twice her age. I bet you anything you like he's married and she's his secret girlfriend and now they're having a sneaky little holiday in Paris."

"Well, so what?" says Hazel, sounding bewildered.

"So my Dad did exactly that. Well, it was just a dirty weekend in Paris, he was probably too mean to go the whole hog with a proper holiday. He took Marianne. You know. Her. And Laura found some French tickets or something afterwards and that's how she first found out he was having an affair."

"Oh, I see," says Hazel uncomfortably. "Still, that's all over now, isn't it? I mean, your Dad's actually married to Marianne and – "

"That doesn't make it better, Hazel. It makes it worse," I snap.

The man's summoning the waiter, paying his bill. The girl gets up and goes to the back of the café, to the *Dames*.

"Won't be a tick," I say, and I go off to the *Ladies* too. She's already in the cubicle. When she comes out I give her a long look. Maybe she's even younger than twenty now I get close up. She washes her hands, glancing over her shoulder at me, looking more nervous than ever.

"Yes, you're worried, aren't you?" I mutter.

She gives a start and sprays water over herself. I give myself a bit of a shock too. I hadn't really meant to say it out loud.

"I know what you're up to – and I think you're mad," I say.

She gasps, going terribly white. For a moment I think she's going to faint. She has to cling to the edge of the wash basin.

"What do you mean?" she says hoarsely.

"Look, I know it's probably not all your fault. I bet he

32

talked you into it. But have you seriously thought of all the trouble you're stirring up?" I say.

She takes hold of me by the shoulders. Her hands are still soaking wet. I can feel her nails digging into me. The water's still rushing into the basin.

"What do you know? Who are you? What do you mean?" she says urgently, and she starts shaking me hard, hurting me.

"Don't! I don't see why you're mad at me. Let me go," I say, and I try to wriggle free.

But she's bigger and stronger than me – and she's in such a state she hardly seems to know what she's doing. She pushes me across the little room, hard up against the door of the lavatory.

"Tell me what you *mean*," she says again, fiercer than ever.

"Nothing!" I gabble. "It was just – seeing you together like that. That man – he even looks like my Dad. And my Dad went off with a girlfriend about your age – he even took her to Paris, the same as you. And then my Mum found out and he walked out on us all. And we don't care now, we're better off without him – but there were all these rows and my little sisters kept on crying and my Mum couldn't even sleep much and – and"

"What are you talking about?" she says, letting me go at last. She shakes her head, as if she can't make sense of my words.

"That's why you're scared, isn't it? Because you don't want anyone to find out about you and that man having an affair?"

She stares at me – and then she seems to take in what I'm saying at long last. She wipes her wet hand over her forehead, letting out her breath in a long sigh.

"Look – just mind your own business, you silly little kid," she says, and then she flounces off.

I stare after her, shaking my own head. She's really

33

weird. I just tried to *talk* to her and she practically went hysterical. Maybe it's her guilty conscience. Although if she really cared that much she wouldn't be here, would she?

I switch off the taps and rub my sore shoulders where she dug her nails in. What a cheek she had, treating me like that. She's lucky I don't have her up for assault.

I go into the lavatory, treading gingerly, because I've been told a lot of funny stories about French loos. I'm expecting a dubious hole in the ground – so it's almost a disappointment when I find a perfectly ordinary lavatory – *and* it's scrupulously clean.

When I rejoin Hazel and the others they're looking very worried.

"Did you wonder what had happened to me, Haze?" I ask.

But they're not fussing about me. They're fussing about the bill the waiter's just plonked down on our table.

"It *can't* be right," says Elaine. "We just had four ice-creams. And this isn't one of the posh touristy cafés where they charge a fortune. It can't really be 80 francs."

"What!" I snatch the bill from her. "That's about eight pounds – for four tiny little ices! It's eight francs, surely – not eighty!"

"It is eighty, Stevie," says Michelle, sighing. She gets out her purse. "I'm not going to have much money left at this rate."

"Me neither," says Hazel. "So what is it each, 20 francs? I've only got a 100 franc note."

"So have I."

"And me."

"Me too. Well, it can't be helped." I take a deep breath and summon the waiter with a lordly wave of one hand. I don't feel very lordly actually. And by the time the waiter is finished with us – and giving us each our

34

separate change – I feel like a very lowly peasant indeed.

"Do you think we ought to give him a tip?" Elaine whispers.

"You must be joking," I say.

"Yes, but what if he expects one? He might get even nastier," says Elaine. "Let's ask that nice man if we ought to."

But Mr Smoothie and his weird girlfriend have gone.

"Do you know, that girl practically beat me up in the loo just now," I say indignantly. "Just over some little thing I happened to say to her."

"There's lots of people get tempted to beat you up, Stevie," says Elaine, with surprising feeling. "Oh thank goodness, look, on the menu, it says service compris. So we don't have to give him anything more."

"Just as well." I say. "At this rate I'm going to run out of money by tomorrow. And I'm *still* starving."

But when we get back to our bedroom Michelle produces a giant bar of Cadbury's milk chocolate and shares it round, which helps considerably.

Breakfast is a bit of a disappointment next morning. I had high hopes of golden croissants and that very fierce black coffee that makes your head jerk when you drink it. No such luck. Madame provides lots of French bread – baguettes – cut up into little chunks, some runny apricot jam, and pots of very weak tea. It's not bad, I suppose, but it's a bit basic – and there's not quite enough. It's particularly annoying when I peer over at the teachers' little table in the corner. *They're* noshing away on croissants. They've got a whole basket full. There are golden crumbs all over Mrs Wainwright's capacious bosom. She doesn't seem at all concerned that we are having vastly inferior fare.

"She's just like Marie Antoinette," I say bitterly. "She doesn't care that we've run out of bread while she's on her third croissant."

"Actually Stevie, when Marie Antoinette said "Let them eat cake" she didn't really mean – " Elaine starts.

"I don't *care* what she really meant," I say. "Don't you ever give it a rest, Elaine?"

She certainly doesn't give it a rest all morning. We get taken on this coach over to the Cité, which is a big island in the Seine. We go to the Conciergerie which is where they kept all the prisoners in the old days. They've actually got Marie Antoinette's cell, and there's a special Women's Courtyard where they could have a little walk – before finding out if it was their turn for the daily trip to the guillotine.

We have this special guide burbling away at one side and Elaine whispering relentlessly right behind me – and I'd give anything for them both to shut up so I could have a little wander by myself and imagine how I'd feel if my hands were tied, my collar ripped open and my hair cut off before being dragged out to the tumbrils.

I look down at the flagstones, wondering how many other feet have walked that way. My head's bent, my neck's vulnerably exposed.

A cold hand suddenly goes *chop* against my neck and I jump violently.

"Terry!"

Terry laughs. "I didn't hurt, did I? I just couldn't resist it. I wish they still had a guillotine on show, I'd love to see what it's really like."

"Oh Terry, you are gruesome," someone simpers. It's Lurking Lucy.

"What sort of noise do you think it makes when they slice through the neck? A bit like chopping carrots? Although there are soft squelchy bits as well as hard bone. More like chopping melons, I suppose. And what about the blood? I bet it would spray everywhere. Those women with their knitting couldn't get too close or they'd get all their woollies dyed scarlet."

Terry appreciates a little ghoulish conversation and we chatter together amicably. We keep each other company going round Notre Dame too. It's a really beautiful cathedral and if they'd only stop *telling* me about it then I'd like to tiptoe round it peacefully. But chance would be a fine thing. I feel sorry for the people on their knees in front of the holy statues, trying to have a quiet pray. How can they concentrate when there are hoards of tourists tramping about, cameras clicking. I gaze up at this wonderful stained glass window and some of Terry's mates barge right into me and I shove back and they squawk – and Mrs Wainwright turns round and glares at me.

"I might have known you'd be the cause of the trouble, Stephanie Day," she hisses.

What a cheek! Well okay, if she thinks I'm trouble I'll live up to my reputation. The guide is telling us all about this book *The Hunchback of Notre Dame* – so I immediately launch into my Quasimodo impersonation. I cross my eyes, scrunch up my nose, let my tongue loll and then I lumber around with one shoulder up so that it looks as if I've got a hump on my back. Terry and his mates fall about laughing and start doing their own imitations. A flock of elderly American tourists squeak nervously and back away.

Mrs Wainwright gets so furious she hisses things that are highly unsuitable for inside a church.

When we get back in the coach she makes me sit next to her. I hunch as far away as possible and make Quasimodo faces to myself.

We get out of the coach again at the Botanical Gardens, where we all get given a special French packed lunch. Madame's idea of a sandwich is hilarious. It's half a French loaf each, stuffed with cheese. You have to open your mouth so wide your jaw aches. I have a shrewd suspicion Mrs Wainwright has false teeth. She doesn't take a proper bite of her sandwich, she just sort of sucks the end. There's a banana too, a drink of fruit juice, and a piece of cherry cake. It's not such a bad lunch actually – but Hazel doesn't seem very interested in hers.

"What's up, Haze?"

"Nothing."

"You're not sulking, are you? It wasn't *my* fault you were by yourself on the coach. I didn't *want* to sit with Mrs Wainwright."

"Yeah, I know."

"So what's up?"

"*Nothing*!"

"Come on, shall I take a photo of you in front of all the flowers? Give us your camera."

But she even seems to have lost interest in her photography. I can't work out what's up with her at all.

"Come on, Stevie. There's a zoo right over there. Let's go and have a look," Terry yells.

"No, you're to stay put," says Mrs Wainwright. "There isn't time to go and look at the zoo. And I think I've seen enough Wild Animal behaviour already today."

She looks at me pointedly and I give her a sickly grin. She lets me sit next to Hazel again when we get back onto the coach.

"The Eiffel Tower next, I can't wait," I say.

Hazel doesn't bother to reply.

Elaine is deep in her guide book again, announcing that there are 1,652 steps up to the top, if anyone fancies climbing up the hard way.

"We'll be taking the lift, Elaine," says Mrs Wainwright.

Elaine tells us that the lifts all have to have special brakes.

"It's going to be great going down in the lifts," I say.

"You know you get a sort of thump in the tummy when a lift goes down a few floors – so it's going to feel incredible swooping all that way downwards, just like something in a fun fair. Hey, Haze, I wonder if the lifts ever get stuck? Hazel?"

Hazel's got her eyes shut. She's gone green again.

"You need another one of your Nan's travel pills," I say.

Hazel doesn't open her eyes again, even though we're driving through some really interesting bits on the Left Bank.

The coach draws up near the Eiffel Tower. Hazel has to open her eyes now – but she's still pale green.

"Maybe it was the cheese sandwich," I say. "Or the cherry cake. Are you actually going to be sick, Hazel? You look as if you are."

"I – I do feel a bit . . ." Hazel whispers. "Maybe – maybe I'd better not go up the Tower, eh? Maybe I ought just to stay on the coach, try and have a little sleep or something."

"But you can't miss going up the Tower, Haze. It's the best bit."

"Yes, but – but I really don't feel well. I'd better not," says Hazel. "Will you tell Mrs Wainwright for me, Stevie?"

So I go and tell her – and she sighs irritably.

"What's all this, Hazel?" she says, pushing her way up the coach.

"I'm ever so sorry but I feel a bit sick, so can I just stay in the coach and – "

"No, of course you can't," says Mrs Wainwright briskly. "The driver wants to lock it up so he can go away for a cup of coffee. And anyway, if you feel sick staying on the stuffy old coach will only make things worse. Come on out in the fresh air. You'll feel as right as rain in no time."

Hazel doesn't look any better when she gets out of the coach. She looks worse. And when we all troop over to the Tower she goes greener than ever.

"I can't, Stevie," she whispers.

"Take some deep breaths. Maybe you'll feel much better when you're up at the top. The air will be really fresh up there."

"I can't go up it," Hazel says desperately. "That's what's making me feel so awful. I'm scared, Stevie."

I stare at her. She really *is* scared, I can see that now. Her eyes are all wide and starey and she's shaking.

"What are you scared *of*, Haze?" I ask. "I mean, it's safe. You're not going to fall off, are you? There are all these barriers. And it can't collapse. All those two and a half million rivets aren't suddenly going to pop out simultaneously."

"I know. But I can't help it, I'm still scared. I've always hated heights. I don't even like looking down from a double decker bus. But I usually shut up about it because people laugh. But it's no use, I just can't go all the way up that tower." She peers right up at the platform at the top, and I can see the sweat standing out on her forehead.

"Okay," I say, because I know there's no point arguing with her. It's like when you have a nightmare and you wake up, your heart pounding. You know perfectly well it was just a dream and you're safe in your own bed – and yet you're still scared out of your wits.

"But what am I going to *do*, Stevie?"

"Tell Mrs Wainwright. And wait at the bottom."

"They won't let me."

"Oh Haze. They can't carry you up bodily, can they?"

"But it's all part of the school trip, we've paid extra . . . Nan *said* I should tell them I didn't want to go, but I thought I'd be all right once I was here. I didn't realize it was going to be so *big*. Oh Stevie, I can't, I just

40

can't."

"Come on. We'll go and tell Mrs Wainwright together and – "

"I can't tell her either, she's been so cross with us already, and she's so *bossy*."

"Then we'll tell Ms Mosely. She's meant to be all sisterly and understanding, isn't she?"

We prise her away from Mr Mason and start explaining. She's not at *all* sisterly or understanding.

"Oh Hazel, don't be such a drip," she says. "Come on, give it a try. You'll feel so proud of yourself when you get to the top. And there's absolutely nothing to be frightened of. We've got to stop being so *feeble*."

"I'll look after you, Hazel," says Mr Mason, and he actually puts his arm around her.

But even this incredible offer from the Beloved can't make Hazel change her mind.

"I can't," she says, and she presses her lips together and screws up her face.

"You're just being childish now," says Ms Mosely.

She thinks Hazel's pulling that face because she's sulking. She isn't. She's trying hard not to cry.

"She can't go up and that's that," I say briskly. "She can just wait here for us."

"No she can't," says Ms Mosely. "We're not having anyone left on their own. Anything could happen. No, I'm sorry, Hazel, but you've simply got to stop being silly and come up with us."

"What about if someone else stays? Would that be all right?" I persist, because I can see Hazel's really desperate.

"Nobody else *wants* to stay here twiddling their thumbs," says Ms Mosely. She clears her throat and calls out, "Does anyone want to stay at the bottom and wait? Hazel here doesn't fancy the idea of going up the tower. Is there anyone else who also wants to miss out?"

I glare at her. She knows the others will tease Hazel now. What a cow! She's got horns coming out her head, a Jersey brown skin, and great pink udders.

"What's up, Hazel? You're not chicken, are you?"

"Hazel's scared, look at her!"

"Hazel won't go up the Eiffel Tower, isn't she a *baby*?"

They're all starting. Well, I'll just have to shut them up.

"I don't want to go up either," I say loudly. "I can't quite see the point. I want to look round Paris properly. You can't *see* it when you're right up there, it just looks like a little tiny ant town. So I'll stay."

There's a whole buzz and chatter, but no one quite dares call me chicken. They know what they'd get if they did.

Ms Mosely doesn't want to leave the two of us, but she can't very well get out of it. Mrs Wainwright confers with her angrily, while Mr Mason tries to act as a peacemaker.

He manages, just.

"You two girls behave yourselves, do you hear?" says Mrs Wainwright. "No wandering off. Don't talk to anyone. Stay right here, do you understand? You're going to be very bored indeed, because we shall be gone a long time. Still, it's your own silly faults."

They troop off — and Hazel looks at me with tears in her eyes.

"Oh Stevie, thanks. But I feel so awful. I know you were looking forward to it so much. You said it was going to be your best bit. You should have gone with the others. Oh Stevie, you are a pal."

"Shut up, Haze. Come on, get your camera out. We might as well take some pictures of the Eiffel Tower now we're here."

Hazel starts snapping away. Five pretty little gypsy

children are watching her. They've got big brown eyes and long tangled hair and colourful ragged clothes. Bangles clink on their skinny brown wrists.

Hazel takes their photo too, and tries to say a few friendly things, like "Bonjour" and "Comment allez vous?" The gypsy children laugh at her and point, their bangles jingling. Hazel laughs at herself too, like a sport. They jostle round her. Hazel's laugh gets a bit uncertain. Then she suddenly shouts.

"My camera!"

One of the gypsy girls has snatched it – and now she's running like the wind!

Four

"Help! Stop her! She's got my camera!" Hazel yells.

No one takes a blind bit of notice. There are hundreds of tourists milling about, lots of them shouting at the tops of their voices. No one bothers to turn to look at Hazel. Nobody even understands what she's saying.

"Oh Stevie, my camera! What's French for thief?" Hazel sobs. "Oh I remember. Voleur. Isn't that it? Help, help, voleur, cette gypsy fille, she's a voleur, she's got my camera!"

It's no use. Superhomme isn't going to come whizzing out of the sky in his red underpants to sort things out. So Hazel will just have to make do with SuperStevie instead.

"Stevie! Stevie, what are you doing?" Hazel yells after me. "Stevie, Mrs Wainwright made us swear to stay right here. You can't run after them! She'll be *furious*!"

But I can. I'm doing just that. Because those kids aren't going to get away with it. That camera means a lot to Hazel. They haven't got much money. It'll be donkey's years before Hazel's Nan gets another win on the Bingo like that. So I'm going to get it back for her. Bother Mrs Wainwright. Who cares if she's cross. She's cross anyway, even when I'm behaving.

"Stevie, wait for me!" Hazel shouts, and she starts panting along behind me.

She'll never keep up. But I can't bother about Hazel

now. I've got to concentrate on those little gypsy girls – especially the one with the camera. They're running so fast. They're all smaller than me and yet they're so quick – and they're so good at dodging in and out of the crowds. And now they're separating – two going that way, one running off down the path, another doubling back towards the tower . . . Which one's got the camera? I don't know! It's not very big and they've all got shawls. It could be hidden anywhere. They might even have dropped it.

One of them turns round, sees me – and laughs. She's openly laughing at me! I'll show her. I charge up to her and she shrieks at her two friends running through the gardens, waving at them to run faster. An old trick! I'm not falling for that.

"I bet you've got it – and you just want me to think the others have!" I shout. I make a supreme effort, catch her up, and pounce on her. She staggers and we both fall over on the path. She yells and punches and kicks while I try to fend her off as best I can, trying to grab at her shawl.

"Gee, will you take a look at that! That girl's bullying that poor little gypsy kiddie! Say, that's a real shame," says one large American matron indignantly.

"I'm not bullying! She's stolen my friend's camera," I yell – but when I pull at her shawl I can only find grubby wool. She can't be hiding it in the thin folds of her ragged dress.

"I've got the wrong one!" I moan.

I don't think she can speak a word of English – but she laughs triumphantly and then spits right in my face.

"You little whatsaname!" I say, giving her a push.

"Will you try picking on someone your own size!" calls another American.

I look round wildly. The other two are still capering about in the gardens, miles away – and the fourth is right over by the tower. Wait a minute. There were five before. Yes, I'm sure there were five. So what's happened to the other one?

The two in the gardens see me hesitating and start shouting and running – but I'm wise to their little tricks now. It's not them. And I don't think it's the one over by the tower either. It's the fifth one, and she's hiding somewhere.

Hazel catches me up, scarlet in the face and gasping.

"Oh Stevie, are you all right? You were fighting with her! Wouldn't she give it back?"

"She hasn't got it. There's another one – a fifth one. You didn't see her?"

"They were all so quick. I didn't even realize what was happening. Oh Stevie, what will Nan say?"

"She's not going to say anything, because I'm going to get it *back* for you," I say, running dementedly up and down the gardens, trying to work it out. Why didn't I see the fifth one? I ran straight after them, and for a while they were all running together . . . No, wait. Maybe she dodged away and I just didn't notice. Maybe she stopped running. Maybe she hid somewhere. Maybe she's still hiding!

I rush round, Hazel stumbling after me, running right back almost to the spot where it happened. There's a line of parked cars and I suddenly dodge round the back of them – and there she is! Squatting there, the camera clutched in her hands.

"Got you!" I yell.

But she's too quick for me. She leaps up, and she's off again, running like mad. But I can run fast too, I'm older than she is, and I'm even more determined. I'll catch her now if it's the last thing I do.

It nearly is too. She charges right across the gardens and out into the street, darting across the road. I run after her, and I forget that French traffic goes the opposite way. I glance to the right and run – and there's a great screech of brakes from my left. Some French bloke starts screaming at me furiously, and if I stayed around to listen I'd most probably increase my vocabulary of French swear words considerably. But I can't stop, I've got to get that camera back – and so I dash off again, Monsieur still bellowing after me.

The gypsy girl's the other side of the road now, darting along the pavement, and then down a side road – but she's not going to dodge me this time. I tear after her, and she turns round and sees me and runs out into the road again, right across and down another avenue opposite.

I stop for the traffic this time, but I realize I might well be stopped for ever, and I'll lose sight of her any minute now, so I grit my teeth and hope for the best. There are more squeals of brakes, more shouts, but I dodge the cars and keep on running, and now I'm on the pavement again, thank God, though my heart's pounding and my legs are as wobbly as jelly.

I have to stop and lean against the wall just for a second or two and then I start running again with renewed determination. I run and I run and I run – and she runs too, but she hasn't had a rest like me, and she's tiring now, slowing down a little. She blunders into a table outside a corner café and stumbles, almost falling. She holds the camera out, and I can tell she's wondering whether to leave it – but she hangs on and hobbles on. She's hurt herself, she's limping, but she's still running as fast as she can.

And I'm running too and it's getting easier now. She must be able to hear the thud of my footsteps as I close in on her. She panics and darts uselessly up one side of the street and suddenly turns and runs down the other side. I cross the road and I'm even nearer, closer and closer, almost there. I run on and reach out and as she turns another corner I catch hold of her by the hem of her skirt. I grip tight, and she staggers and then falls.

I'm onto her, sitting on top of her thin little body, grabbing at her wrist so she has to loosen her tight grip on the camera at last.

"Got you!" I say.

She squirms and wriggles but there's nothing she can do. I keep my head out of the way in case she spits like her little friend. But she's too tired, too scared. Her eyes are swivelling round desperately, and I can see the tears welling up.

It makes me feel awful – as if it's somehow my fault. She's gabbling something in French but I don't understand a word of it.

"I'm English," I say. "Je ne comprends pas. Er – vous êtes une méchante fille, do you know that? Oui, très méchante."

She doesn't seem to understand me either. She starts crying properly, tears spilling down her brown cheeks.

"You're just trying to make me feel sorry for you," I say.

But it's working. "Okay," I say, sighing, and I ease myself off her. "Okay, I'll let you go this time. "Compris? Allez vous en. Oui?"

Her eyes open even wider – and then she's up and off in a flash. And as she goes her little hand reaches out and blow me, she tries to take another swipe at the camera! But I hang on and she gives up and rushes off, still limping, tears still streaming down her face.

I stare after her, shaking my head. Ah well. I've got Hazel's camera back. That's really all that matters.

She'll be so pleased when she sees me. I wonder actually where she is. And where am I, come to that? I peer round, staring up and down the strange street, not even remembering which way I was running. I don't know. I suddenly shiver. I'm lost. I'm lost somewhere in a strange foreign city and I don't know what to do.

I look round helplessly. When we were little Laura always impressed upon us that we should find a policeman if ever we were lost. So I look round for a gendarme but there isn't one in sight. And what should I ask him, anyway? What's "Can you tell me the way back to the Eiffel Tower?" in French?

Hang on. My head suddenly clears. I look up. Right up. Above the buildings. And there, high in the sky, is the unmistakable gigantic pointing finger of the Eiffel Tower. What an idiot I am. That's all I have to do. Keep an eye on it, and walk towards it!

I set off at a brisk pace, the camera clutched to my chest. I turn the corner, walk down the road – and there's the café with the tables, where the little gypsy girl stumbled. There's a little crowd outside, a circle of excited French people surrounding someone. The someone seems to be crying.

"J'ai perdu mon amie Stevie," the someone sobs.

"Hazel?"

She bobs out between two large French ladies.

"Oh Stevie! I lost you – and I didn't know what to do. I tried so hard to keep up but you run so fast and I had this awful stitch – and *you've got my camera back*!" She gives a great squeal and throws her arms around me.

All the French onlookers laugh and exclaim with a Gallic sense of occasion. The fattest lady can speak a little English and asks us exactly what happened. I tell her about the little gypsy gang and she says something in French and everyone shakes their heads and sighs expressively.

"These children, they are everywhere. There is nothing our police can do, because they are too little."

She makes it sound as if all the gendarmes are too little, and I can't help picturing a tiny toddler size police force on trikes – but doubtless I make far funnier mistakes when I try to speak French.

"But you got the camera! How did you manage?" she asks.

"I ran after them," I say.

"She ran for miles," says Hazel, wiping her eyes and smiling at me proudly. "I couldn't keep up, but Stevie never gives up. She got my camera back for me."

They all start clapping me on the back and telling me I'm formidable. I beam at everyone. This is all very pleasant.

It gets even more pleasant when the proprietor of the café comes out with two enormous ice-cream sundaes and presents them to us with a flourish. Although . . . are they expecting us to pay for them?

"Oh dear – lovely, très belle, but – but nous n'avons pas beaucoup d'argent," I say, although my hand's reaching out for the magical ice-cream all by itself. There are almonds and cherries and little peachy bits and at least three flavours of ice-cream.

The proprietor smiles and burbles away in French. He's obviously saying the French equivalent of "It's on the house."

So Hazel and I sit down at one of the tables and start spooning away, while our audience smiles and nods at us. I'm beginning to be very glad indeed those little girls stole the camera. And I'm beginning to feel very fond of the French too. They can certainly rustle up some splendid ice-creams. Goodness knows what this little lot would cost if last night's plain stawberry ices were so expensive. Still, we're not paying, so why worry.

Hazel is still looking a bit worried all the same.

"We'd better get back soon, Stevie," she says anxiously. "We've been gone ever such a long time. It would be awful if they're down from the tower already and waiting around for us. Mrs Wainwright will be so furious."

"Oh, Hazel, can't you ever relax?" I say, discovering a wonderful ball of blackcurrant ice-cream nestling at the bottom of my glass. "They'll be ages, they *said* they would. Have you got blackcurrant too? Mine's got real fruit in it." I gave the proprietor an enormous smile. "Délicieux!" I proclaim, and I kiss my fingers in that showy-offy French way to prove my appreciation. "Merci beaucoup, Monsieur."

He chuckles delightedly, and kisses his fingers back at me.

"Hey, I'm onto a good thing here," I say.

"You've got blackcurrant stuck in your front teeth," Hazel says. "Come on, Stevie, we really must get back."

"In a minute! Let me finish my wonderful ice-cream first."

I'm so appreciative that Monsieur gives me a little taste of all the different flavours in his ice-cream cabinet and I rave about each one. When we set off at last there's great handshaking all round, and I even get a kiss on each cheek.

"I wonder if the French police force takes foreigners?" I muse. "I think I'd rather like to live here when I grow up."

"I wouldn't. It's all so strange and different," says Hazel.

"That's what I like."

"I felt so awful when I couldn't find you. When I thought I was lost," says Hazel, and her voice goes shaky remembering.

"Honestly Hazel! How could you possibly think you were lost? You've only got to look up and get your bearings by the Eiffel Tower," I say loftily. I look up at it myself and give it a little wave. "There! I wonder if they're up there, waving back?"

"We've been gone such ages – I think they'll be waiting, absolutely fuming," says Hazel.

But when we get back to the spot where they left us there's no sign of them.

"There! I told you not to worry," I say cheerily.

We wait. And we wait and we wait. And then we see a school party trooping back from the Tower.

"Come on, it's them," I say – but when we get a bit nearer we see it isn't them at all, it's another school entirely.

"Funny," I say. "I wonder what's happened to our lot."

One of the teachers in charge of their school is looking at us suspiciously.

"Are you girls English?" she asks. "You're not the two missing from the Clarence School, are you?"

"We're from Clarence, yes," I say. "But we're not missing."

"Your teachers think you are! When our coach arrived they were rushing round having kittens trying to find you two."

"Oh no," says Hazel, going white.

"They waited half an hour apparently – but then they had to complete the coach tour."

"Oh well, we'll catch them up," I say, trying to sound jaunty. "Where were they going next?"

"The Hotel des Invalides – but you'd better not try going after them, you'll get lost again. Your teachers said if by any chance we found you to tell you to go straight back to your hotel and wait there. Have you got enough money for a Metro ticket?"

We nod.

"You really are thoughtless and irresponsible, you know. Your poor teachers were so worried about you."

She drones on and on. Hazel looks as if she's near to tears.

"It wasn't really our fault, Miss. These gypsy girls stole my camera. Stevie, my friend here, she went after

52

them and – "

I prepare to take up the tale, but this teacher isn't the slightest bit interested.

"You save your excuses for your own teachers," she says snidely. "Off you go now."

"Oh dear – I feel this is all my fault," says Hazel, as we walk off. "If it hadn't been for me not wanting to go up the Eiffel Tower – "

"We wouldn't have this lovely free afternoon to explore Paris!" I interrupt eagerly.

"Stevie! We can't. We've got to go straight back to the hotel."

"How are they going to know? Their coach trip lasts right up until tea-time, we were told. So what's the point in going back to the hotel and twiddling our thumbs? Let's see a bit while we're here. I know what I want to do."

"What?"

"Find the sewers!"

"No. Definitely not. I can't. Stevie!"

But I've stopped a likely looking bloke and I'm in the middle of asking.

"Excusez-moi Monsieur, mais ou sont les égouts? Vous savez? Égouts." I mime disgust and hold my nose. "Avec beaucoup de rats."

"Ah oui!" He understands! He tells me that they're not far away, near the Pont de l'Alma.

I thank him effusively and give Hazel a big nudge.

"There! I'm getting really fluent. Pont, that's a bridge. This way."

"Stevie, I can't go in a sewer. I'd almost sooner go up the Eiffel Tower than go down a sewer. I'll do anything else, I swear I will, but please please please, not the sewer."

"You can wait outside. And hang on to your wretched camera this time."

We find the sewers easily enough – but to my immense disappointment they are Fermés. They're only open between two and five on Mondays and Wednesdays and the occasional Saturday and, curses curses, this is Tuesday.

"What a pity," says Hazel, sighing with relief.

"You're telling me. Oh well. Que sera sera. What will be will be. Get that. I'm multi-lingual now. So let's just wander and see what we find, eh?"

I tuck my hand into Hazel's arm and we walk on. I feel all light-headed and springy and free. The river Seine sparkles green-grey in the sunlight. My eyes sparkle green-grey in my face. Freedom!

And then we see a signpost to the Hotel des Invalides and decide to walk as far away as quickly as possible. We don't really fancy an unexpected encounter with our own school party.

"Poor things, I bet they're bored stiff," I say. "Let's cross over to the Right Bank, Haze, and then there's no chance of bumping into anyone we know."

So we go over the Pont de la Concorde and have a stroll round the Jardin des Tuileries. Lots of other people are strolling round too. Hazel oohs and aahs over the sweet little French toddlers in their funny formal clothes. Then some boys about our age circle round us and start saying daft things. I don't actually understand, but you can tell they're rude. I say some short sharp things in English and they all crease up and imitate me.

"There! This is what school trips should be about. Communication with the natives," I say. "I'm getting ever so thirsty, Hazel. I think it was all that ice-cream. How much do you think they'd charge for a coke here?"

"Too much," says Hazel, but she comes with me to the Rue de Rivoli to have a look.

There are some lovely looking cafés but a quick glance at the menus tells me that Hazel is only too right. And then I see an amazing shop. Amazing for the middle of Paris, that is. It's a great big branch of *W. H. Smiths*!

"It really is the English bookshop! And look, it says there's an English tea-room too. We can have a coke in there."

"No we can't," says Hazel, reading the menu on the outside door. "It's all different – and ever so posh. Hey Stevie, you'll never guess how much they charge for an English bun! I don't believe it!"

I don't believe it either. I've spotted someone I know, standing around inside, looking at the English newspapers. It's that man who helped us order the strawberry ices, the one who looks like my Dad, the one with the maniac girfriend.

"Look who it isn't," I say, nudging Hazel.

He's glancing at his watch, frowning.

"He's obviously waiting for someone. Her. Dirty old man," I say scathingly.

"You don't know," says Hazel.

Mr Smoothie is suddenly joined by the oddest looking scruffy little man, not at all his type. They start conversing rapidly.

"There!" says Hazel. "You were wrong. Ha ha."

"They look awfully suspicious, don't they?" I say. "I wonder what they're nattering on about? Look at the way the little one keeps looking over his shoulder. He doesn't half look guilty. And even Mr Smoothie looks a bit hot and bothered. They look like two criminals fixing up some kind of shady deal."

I stop – and my words ring significantly in my own ears.

Five

I stare at Hazel excitedly.

"Two crooks," I say. "Yes. It's obvious."

"No it's not," says Hazel. "They're just two ordinary men having a chat together."

"Oh come on! Just *look* at the little scruffy one."

"All right, he's a bit untidy – "

"And Mr Smoothie's ultra sleek and smart, right? So you're not telling me the two men are ordinary business friends? Neighbours? Relations? They're *crooks*, Haze. It's written all over them. C-R-O-O-K. Don't you ever watch any television?"

"I think you watch too much," says Hazel. "Stevie? Where are you going?"

"I'm going to go in the shop, see if I can overhear anything."

"Oh Stevie, don't! Please! Remember the student and his sausages. You were wrong then, weren't you?"

"A detective can't be right all the time. I'm not claiming to be superhuman," I say airily. "But I have an *instinct* about these matters, Hazel."

"So have I," says Hazel, and she sighs heavily. "My instinct tells me this spells trouble. T-R-O-U- "

But before she's finished spelling it out I slip into *Smiths*, determined to prove I'm right. And even if I'm wrong – which I'm sure I'm not – it won't do any harm if I polish up my eavesdropping techniques.

I don't go straight up to them and stand beside them. Credit me with some sense and subtlety. I go over to the magazines and pretend to flick through some boring beauty book. I strain my ears but I can't hear a thing from here. I'm terrified they'll finish their conversation soon and rush off, but I can't be in too much of a hurry or they'll get suspicious already. Hazel is lurking in the doorway, biting her lip anxiously and staring straight at them.

I pull frantic faces at her because she's giving the whole game away. She looks wounded and turns her back on me. But I can't bother about Hazel going all huffy. I've got to concentrate on the two men.

I return the beauty book to the rack and very very casually idle over towards the newspapers. I select one of the big boring ones and peer at the headline as if I really care about the current political situation. I even shake my head occasionally and crinkle my eyebrows.

And all the while I'm trying hard to see if I can hear what they're saying now. They're mumbling cautiously so it's very difficult. They're certainly not talking as if they're ordinary friends or acquaintances. They sound as if they're telling each other very special secrets. Only I still can't *quite* catch what they're saying.

I edge closer still, opening up the newspaper so that they'll think I'm truly engrossed in catching up on the English news.

"Prenez garde," says Mr Smoothie to his furtive companion.

Oh no. Just my luck. They're talking *French*. The scruffy one jabbers something, sounding excited and upset. He waves his arms about a bit, nearly catching the edge of my newspaper. I try hard but I can't make sense of a single thing he says, I can't even divide the garble of sounds into separate words. I suppose it's because he's French and speaking with the proper accent. It's easier

57

when Mr Smoothie says something. His French is much slower and sounds more precise.

"A votre aise," he says. "Calmez-vous."

I *get* it! He's trying to calm Mr Scruffy down a bit. He's not having that much success. Mr Scruffy gabbles away. Mr Smoothie nods and says soothingly "Oui, oui."

I've got that bit! Instant translation! Mr Scruffy is off again. I think he's asking some kind of question because his voice rises emphatically.

"Pourquoi croyez-vous que j'aie la jeune fille?" says Mr Smoothie.

La jeune fille! The young girl. Does he mean the girl in the café? The girl who's so crazy about him, judging by the way she was staring up at him.

"C'est bien *elle* qui va courir les risques, pas moi," says Mr Smoothie, and when I glance at him there's a little smile quivering his lips.

Elle. That means she. The girl. And it's not difficult to suss out what les risques might be. So, she's taking the risks, not him. And he's *smiling* about it. What an absolute cochon. His face grows pinker and his nose snoutier as I stare.

Maybe I'm staring a little bit too much. Mr Smoothie suddenly looks up and sees me. I quickly return to my paper, turning a page, moving my lips as if I'm reading it intently.

"Rapprochez-vous, la gosse écoute, n'est-ce pas?" Mr Smoothie whispers.

I think he's talking about me! I'm the gosse, whatever that is. It doesn't sound very flattering.

They're talking away together now, in such low rapid French it's harder than ever to make out what they're saying.

"Dites à votre gars, elle va lui attendre demain. Compris? Sous les rats."

Under the *rats*? The girl is going to be under the rats

demain – that's tomorrow.

Mr Scruffy nods and says something that sounds like Mimi. Mr Smoothie whispers it too. Perhaps it's the girl's name?

And then he suddenly says something louder, sounding suspicious.

"Qui est elle?"

"Laquelle?"

"Celle-ci! Je l'ai déjà vue quelquepart!"

Oh help! They're talking about me. I don't like the way they're looking at me. Mr Smoothie's obviously wondering where he's seen me before. I think it's time to make a hasty retreat.

I dodge round them and rush towards the shop doorway. I hear someone calling after me and rush even faster.

"Stevie!" Hazel's bright red in the face. "Stevie, what are you *doing*? The shop people are shouting at you. They think you're stealing the newspaper!"

Oh no! I'd forgotten I was holding it! I've mangled it all up too.

The sales assistant sees I'm English and talks to me severely in my own language.

"I think you had better pay for the newspaper, Miss."

"But – but I was just looking at it. I don't really want to buy it. I don't even like newspapers," I say, doing my best to smooth it out.

It stays resolutely crumpled.

"I don't think anyone else will want to buy it now," says the assistant. "That will be twelve francs, please."

I don't believe it! Over a pound for a newspaper I don't even want – and it doesn't cost anywhere near that at home. But I don't really want to start an international incident and so I fumble in my purse and pay up.

"Idiot," Hazel hisses.

"Where've they gone, Haze? Mr Smoothie and Mr

59

Scruffy?" I ask her urgently.

"I don't know. They were there a minute ago. But then I got distracted by you stealing the newspaper and – "

"You should have watched to see where they went. We should be following them."

"We?" says Hazel.

"Only maybe it's just as well they've disappeared. I think Mr Smoothie recognized me – and he didn't look too happy about it. Haze, I was right. He *is* a crook. No listen, I'm not kidding around this time."

I take hold of her arm and we start walking along the Rue de Rivoli.

"Well what sort of crook is he? He doesn't *look* like one. He's too posh," says Hazel.

"Exactly. He's careful not to do any of the dirty work, take any of the risks himself. I heard him say so. You know who's going to do it all for him?"

"That little scruffy man?"

"Well, he's obviously involved too – but Mr Smoothie said it was the girl who was going to take the risks, that she'd do it."

"Do what?"

"Well. I'm not quite sure. They were speaking French, Haze, it was jolly difficult to understand."

"Are you sure you didn't just get hold of the wrong end of the stick? You keep on making things up. First you had Mr Smoothie and his girl having an affair, and now you say they're criminals – "

"Here! I've just thought! Those things I said to the girl last night, in the ladies loo. I went on about her looking worried and that she should think twice and not let herself get talked into it. I was meaning an affair. But she obviously thought I meant this criminal deal, whatever it is. *That's* why she went beserk and practically beat me up."

"What are you *on* about, Stevie?" says Hazel, yawning. "I'm getting a bit fed up of you. I *know* you keep making it all up. You just like being daft and playing detective. But it's just a game. You can't kid me. Let's shut up about those two boring men and look in the shop windows, eh?"

She saunters on, up the arcade. I take a deep breath, wondering how on earth I'm going to convince her this time. And then Mr Smoothie steps out from behind one of the shop pillars and grabs hold of me!

"I think you and I had better have a few words, young lady," he says. His voice is low but there's a terrifying menace in his tone. He's got hold of me by the wrists, his fingers pressing so hard that my pulse jumps underneath.

"What do you mean?" I stammer.

The scruffy man's gone. It's just the two of us – and Hazel, who's wandering on, peering into a clothes shop window, utterly oblivious.

"You're the kid that was in the café last night. And now here you are again, creeping around after me. What's your little game, eh? Why are you so interested in me?"

"I'm not! Let me go."

"Oh no. I think you and I have got a bit of plain talking to do," he says, and he gives a vicious pull on my wrists, bending one of my arms right back. "Come with me, little girl. We're going to have a chat in my car."

"Help!" I yell at the top of my voice.

"Shut up! You shout once more and I'll really get angry," he threatens, pulling me along.

But Hazel's heard me, though she doesn't spot me for a moment.

"Stevie? Stevie, I *know* you're messing about. You can't fool me," she calls – and then she sees me struggling with the man and her mouth drops open.

I wouldn't blame her if she ran off. But she doesn't.

"What are you doing to my friend?" she cries tugging at Mr Smoothie's arm. "Leave go of her!"

"Push off, you," he says curtly, though he looks nonplussed to see there are two of us.

"No I won't! I'll – I'll call my teachers if you don't watch out! Stop pulling her like that."

My eyes swim with stupid tears. I try to blink them back – and then suddenly see they might be an advantage. I open my eyes wide open and let the tears start rolling down my cheeks.

"I don't know why you're being so horrible to me," I say, in as silly a little-girly voice as I can manage. If only Carla were here, she'd be so much more convincing. "I thought you looked so nice – just like my Dad – he went off and left us – I've hardly seen him since – I thought you *were* him just at first – "

"What are you talking about?" he says impatiently.

"That's why I got so close to you back in the shop. I wanted to stand next to you. Pretend you were my Dad," I whimper in a nauseating fashion.

"Well, what were you meaning when you spoke to – to my lady friend last night?"

"I don't like her. She's like the girl my Dad went off with," I wail.

"Look, what is all this stupid nonsense about your father? You're telling me a pack of lies," he says – but he doesn't sound certain.

"It's true," says Hazel hurriedly. "Her Dad left them, he went off with this girl Marianne – and he does look ever so like you."

"So is *that* what all this nonsense has been about?" he says – and he sounds irritated – but very relieved too. "Stupid kids. Grow up, can't you? Now rush off back to your teachers and don't come creeping after me again – or there'll be trouble, do you hear?"

He gives me a final shake and then stalks off. I wipe my cheeks quickly. My hand's trembling like anything.

"Oh Stevie," Hazel whispers, and she's shaking too.

"I wasn't really crying," I say quickly. "I was just putting it on to kid him."

"I know. You were ever so clever."

"And you were quite brave, Haze, coming back like that. Thanks," I say, and I give her arm a squeeze.

"It was so awful when I saw the way he'd got hold of you. He's so horrible. The way he was looking at you – he didn't seem to care what he did, he just wanted to shut you up. Oh Stevie – you don't think he'd have - have *murdered* you, do you?"

"Of course not. Now who's getting carried away?" I say – although the thought had occurred to me too. He was so strong and he really hurt my wrists. I rub them, wincing a little. "I'm going to have a line of little bruises on both of them, where his fingers dug in," I say.

"I feel so awful, not believing you before. I didn't realize. He *is* a crook, Stevie. You're right, he's something really big and evil. And he *was* obviously planning something bad."

"Something that's going to happen tomorrow. Something involving that girlfriend. I think she's going to meet the scruffy man, or someone else, at this special place. Under the rats."

"Under the *rats*?"

"Yes, I know. It doesn't make sense, does it? Do you think he means the sewers? They're open tomorrow, aren't they? Between two and five, that notice said. If *only* they'd said a time for this rendez-vous tomorrow."

"You're sure they didn't?"

"Not that I heard. How do you say it in French – à neuf heures, à dix heures – I didn't hear anything like that. They just said this girl would be under the rats tomorrow. And then they said her name. Mimi."

63

"Mimi?"

"Well, something like that. I *think* it was her name."

"Oh Stevie! Maybe it wasn't Mimi. Maybe it was *midi*. You know. That's how the French say twelve o'clock. It's like our midday."

"Of course! There! So they're meeting up at twelve tomorrow morning – under the rats. It can't be the sewers then. That place was locked up like a fortress. And anyway, how could you be under the rats? Not unless you lay down in all the gunge and let them run all over you."

"Shut up!"

"Well, we've simply got to suss this out, Haze. We've got to stop them."

"Stevie!" Hazel takes hold of me by the wrists.

"Don't, they're still ever so sore from where that brute mauled at me."

"Exactly! You're right, Stevie. This isn't a game. We can't keep on getting involved. That man was so frightening when he thought you suspected something. Now we've just about managed to convince him that it was all a mistake, and you were just hanging round him because you're missing your Dad so much – "

"Yuck yuck yuck," I say. "I wish I hadn't said that now."

"Well, it worked. That's the point. So he stopped trying to drag you off with him. But if we start trailing after him again and he sees us then anything could happen. If he's involved in something really big and dangerous – "

"I think it's smuggling."

"What sort of smuggling? Gold?"

"Gold! They're not expecting that girl to stuff several hundred gold bars down her jumper and up her knicker leg! No. Drugs, stupid. A little tiny packet of heroin or cocaine can be worth an absolute fortune. That's what it'll be. Drugs."

"Well, all right. Drugs. Whatever. So it's dangerous, and if that man sees you and knows you're on to him then he really could try to murder you. *Or me*."

I sigh. Because I know Hazel's right. And I know what I've got to do. My friend Cathy Cope, the detective, has drummed it into me enough times. "Don't ever try to solve anything by yourself, Stevie," she says. "I'd come unstuck if I tried to work that way. I always team up with my colleagues. You can't do this job trying to grab the glory for yourself."

So I suppose I'd better start co-operating with colleagues. Telling the old gendarmes all about Mr Smoothie.

"Okay Haze. We'll go to the nearest police station, tell them all about it," I say.

Hazel looks enormously relieved.

"That's what my Nan always says. If ever you find yourself in trouble, go and look for a policeman. What's French for police station? We'd better ask someone."

"I don't know. Station is Gare, isn't it?" I tug at the sleeve of a French lady. "Excusez-moi, Madame, mais où est la Gare de Gendarmes?"

She stares at me blankly. So do several other passers-by, even when I try doing a helpful little charade, bending my knees and going *'Allo 'Allo 'Allo*. And just when I'm about to give up I suddenly spot a magnificent gendarme standing at the corner of the road.

"He'll do," I say. "He's obviously not a detective, but he can pass it all on to his colleagues, can't he?" I advance, beaming. He doesn't look a very friendly policeman. Perhaps it's the peaked cap of his uniform. It makes him hold his head at a very arrogant angle.

"You don't speak English by any chance, do you?" I ask hopefully.

"Non," he snaps.

Which is a rather daft reply when you come to think of

it, because he must be able to speak a *little* English to understand what I was on about. But anyway. I'd better have a go in French.

"Nous sommes en trouble," I say. "Il y a un méchant homme. Je ne sais pas son nom. Je l'appelle Mr Smoothie. Il est un criminal. Peut-être un drug smuggler. Vous comprenez? Drugs. Heroin. Cocaine. That sort of thing. Ou peut-être il smuggle les bijoux. Je ne sais pas. Mais je *do* sais qu'il est très très méchant et demain cette fille, his accomplice, elle a un rendez-vous avec les autres criminals, à midi, mais je ne sais pas *où*. Il dit sous les rats. Mais *quels* rats? Où sont ces rats? Savez-vous, Monsieur?" I stop, exhausted with all this brilliant French conversation.

The policeman looks a bit tired too. And there's a definite frown on his face.

"Oh help – do you think he understood a word I was saying?" I ask Hazel. "Maybe you'd better have a try. Only your French is worse than mine."

"Which isn't saying much," says Hazel, rather unkindly. "Stevie, he looks so cross. Maybe we'd better give up. He doesn't seem to *want* to understand."

"But he's got to understand!" I say. I turn to him again. "Monsieur Gendarme, c'est un matter de la vie ou la mort. Je suis un detective aussi. Vraiment. Chez nous, en Angleterre, j'ai une très bonne amie Cathy Cope qui est a policeman – I don't know how you say it, gendarmette? – et tous les gendarmes dans notre ville pensent que je suis une très bonne detective . . ." My voice trails away. He's turned his back on me! He's not even bothering to listen any more.

"Come on, Stevie," Hazel hisses.

But I can't give up now. "Écoute, s'il vous plaît," I say, tugging at his uniform.

He whips round and swats my hand as if it's a particularly irritating insect.

"Va-t'en," he commands.

That means go away. Hazel is pulling at me. And perhaps she's wise. He has a holster in his hip. You don't really argue with people with guns.

"Quel cochon," I say fiercely.

"Sh! He'll hear!"

"Good. Well. We'll just have to try another policeman, that's all. They can't all be that unfriendly and uncooperative, surely?"

We walk on purposefully until we spot another. He's in the middle of the road directing traffic.

"Stevie, I really don't think we should bother him – not when he's so busy – " Hazel says. "Stevie? Oh Stevie!"

I thread my way through the traffic and go right up to him. I start telling him but do you know what he does? Starts blowing his silly little whistle at me! Right in my face.

"What else did your mother give you for Christmas?" I enquire – but in an undertone, just in case this one *can* speak English.

I still won't give up. Maybe it will be third time lucky. So we wander on until we see the familiar uniform once more. I waylay him and start my story in my imaginative version of the French language.

He interrupts before I've said very much.

"You lost?"

"No. Well, maybe we are a bit actually, our hotel's near the Arc de Triomphe and I haven't got a clue how you get back there, but never mind that now – "

He gives us highly involved Metro instructions about how to get there, nevertheless.

"Yes, thank you, we'll go back there shortly, but first – *please* listen, it's so wonderful you can actually speak English – let me tell you about these criminals and this deal they're doing tomorrow, under the rats somewhere,

I don't know what that means, do you? I mean, how can you be *under* rats? But I know that's what they said, okay, I got a bit mixed up with my mimis and my midis, but they definitely said sous les rats . . ."

He's looking very perplexed.

"I'm not sure he speaks all that much English," whispers Hazel.

I get to the end of my story and wait. He waits too. And then he smiles uncertainly.

"Good joke," he says. "Now goodbye."

"No, it isn't a *joke*. It's all true, I swear it is. Please believe me. Look, I'll start the whole story again from the beginning – "

"No more funny stories. Goodbye," he says, and he walks away.

"Well. At least he was quite jolly about it," says Hazel. "Come on, Stevie. We *must* get back now. Oh gosh, what's Mrs Wainwright going to say to us? She'll kill us."

"No she won't. Not if we tell her the *truth*," I say, with heavy irony.

"She's not going to believe us either, is she?" says Hazel anxiously.

"No. We'll tell the truth and she'll scream and shout that we're telling her a pack of lies – and *then* she'll kill us.

Six

Mrs Wainwright is waiting when we get back to the hotel at last. She's sitting white-faced on the edge of a chair, while Madame is fussing round her, trying to make her drink a cup of "restoring" English tea. Mrs Wainwright sees us – and spills half the tea into her lap.

"Oh help," I hiss to Hazel. "Now we're for it."

But she doesn't start shouting and screaming. She just sits there, tea dripping down her skirt. She doesn't say anything at all. She just makes an odd little clashing sound and then hurriedly wipes her eyes.

Hazel and I are horrified. We stammer out apologies and I try to start my Mr Smoothie story but she just shakes her head wearily and waves us away. We creep off up the stairs.

"She was *crying*," says Hazel, sounding awed. "Do you think it was because of us – or was it just the hot tea in her lap?"

"Possibly a combination," I say. "But I'm not complaining. We've got off lightly, all things considered."

But that's not the end of it. Mr Mason comes thundering down the stairs, catches us just as we're whisking into our room – and, oh boy, he certainly makes up for Mrs Wainwright. He shouts. He screams. He positively *roars*.

"Do you realize we've been out of our minds with

worry over you. Poor Mrs Wainwright's been in a terrible state, as she's in overall charge of our party.

She didn't know whether to send out search-parties or what. We've already been in touch with the French police, telling them to keep a careful look out for you both –"

"Well, they're not very efficient, because I've been talking to *three* of them, and they weren't the slightest bit interested in us, were they, Haze?" I say.

"Be quiet, Stevie. I've just about had enough of you and your nonsense. I know perfectly well you're the bad influence on poor old Hazel here. She'd never have had the nerve to go off by herself without you."

"Oh Sir – that's not fair, Sir," says Hazel, loyally, although it costs her dear to argue with her beloved. "It wasn't Stevie's fault at all. It was all mine. You see, my camera got stolen and Stevie ran after these gypsy girls to get it back, and then we – well, we had the ice-creams but we couldn't really refuse because they were being so kind to us – and then you weren't there when we got back so well, we were *sort* of making our way back to the hotel when Stevie saw Mr Smoothie – this man, he's a criminal and – "

"*I'll* explain, Hazel," I say hurriedly, because somehow she doesn't sound very convincing.

So I launch into the whole story, giving a superb imitation of both Mr Smoothie and Mr Scruffy to show Mr Mason exactly what they're like – but he's not looking impressed. And then when I'm in the very middle of the Mr Smoothie jumping out from behind the pillar and attacking Stevie scene he interrupts curtly.

"No more amateur dramatics, thanks very much, Stevie." He doesn't sound grateful. "I don't find you very funny, do you know that? It's perfectly obvious you're making the whole thing up. We actually *heard* you say earlier that you wanted to go off and explore

Paris by yourself. And that's what you chose to do. I daresay this whole business of Hazel being afraid to go up the Eiffel Tower was a put-up job. I'm very disappointed in you, Hazel."

"Oh Sir," says Hazel, hanging her head.

"And as for you, Stevie – I've always known you were mischievous and irresponsible – but I didn't think you'd turned into an inveterate liar. I warn you – if there's any more trouble from you two this holiday you'll be very very sorry indeed."

He goes off down the stairs and we creep into our room. Elaine and Michelle are sitting on their beds wide-eyed. They've obviously been eavesdropping.

"Where did you two *get* to?" says Michelle. "They've all been so worried about you."

"Mrs Wainwright was in such a state when we got back to the hotel and you two still weren't here that Madame wanted to call a doctor," says Elaine.

"It wasn't our fault," I say furiously. I'm still smarting from being called a liar. I don't tell lies. I might embroider the truth occasionally, just to make life more interesting, but I never lie.

Hazel's crying.

"He says he's very disappointed in me," she sobs.

"Oh who cares what he thinks," I say.

"I care," Hazel sniffles.

The door bursts open – and it's Ms Mosely now, come to do *her* little bit. She looks very cross but when she sees Hazel's face she softens. She sits on the bed beside Hazel and puts her arm around her.

"Come on, Hazel. It's all over now. You and Stevie behaved like a pair of thoughtless idiots but it's not the end of the world, you know."

"Mr Mason said . . ."

"Don't worry what Mike said. He was just angry because he's been so worried about you, scared that

71

something might have happened to you."

"Something did happen," I say coldly.

"Oh Stevie. Not another one of your preposterous stories," says Ms Mosely.

I decide to save my breath. I stand and glower at Ms Mosely and Hazel acting all girly-girly together – and breathe a sigh of relief when she gets up and goes at last.

"I can't stick her. At least you know where you are with Mrs Wainwright and Mr Mason. She's just so smug and smarmy."

"I think she's quite nice," says Hazel. "So he's called Mike. It suits him, don't you think?"

"Hazel! Don't you *mind* that they think we're telling a pack of lies?" I say furiously.

"Oh come on, Stevie," says Elaine. "You don't seriously expect people to believe all that garbage about Mr Smoothie and Mr Scruffy. It sounded like something straight out of a comic strip."

"I don't remember saying anything of the sort to you, Elaine the Pain. You must have extremely large and waggly Dumbo ears. Now I'll thank you to keep your trunk out of our business. I want to talk to my friend in private, *if* you don't mind."

Elaine retires into her guide book in a huff. Michelle pretends to be busy reading too. I start whispering to Hazel but it doesn't work. If I whisper loud enough for her to hear then Elaine can too. If I lower my voice to a secrets-only tone then Hazel keeps screwing up her face and going "Eh? I can't *hear* you, Stevie."

So I drag her out into the corridor and whisper to her there.

"I can't stand them thinking we're liars, Haze. It's so awful. I'm going to *make* them believe us."

"But how on earth can you do that?" Hazel asks warily.

"We'll have to get evidence."

72

"This conversation has a grimly familiar feel," says Hazel, sighing.

"They are criminals. We *know* that something big is going to happen at twelve midday tomorrow, right? All we have to do is work out *where*. And we've got this whopping great rat clue."

"Don't talk about whopping great rats," says Hazel, shuddering.

"We're going to work it out somehow, Haze. Just you and me."

"Oh no. Listen Stevie – "

"*You* listen. I've tried telling everyone else. And they keep calling me a liar. So we've just got to act by ourselves, right?"

"Wrong. Dead dead wrong. And that's what *we'll* end up if we go after those crooks. Dead."

"We're not going to tackle them ourselves. What do you take me for? Do you think I'm going to round them all up with a toy water pistol? No, don't worry, we're going to keep right out of the way. All we need is to find out where they're meeting – and then hide quite a long way off, out of sight, okay? And then when something actually happens – they hand over the drugs or the jewels or whatever – I give you a nudge and you bob up and take a quick snap with your camera. Simple."

"You must think *I'm* simple if you think I'll agree to that!"

"All right. *I'll* take the photo. I don't mind a bit. I just thought you'd want your little moment of glory because it's your camera, that's all. But suit yourself."

"You're not going to take the photo either, Stevie. Because we're not going. It's far too dangerous – and you know it is. You know what that Mr Smoothie's like. You don't fool around with men like him. You're just so mad at the teachers you're willing to risk anything."

"That's right."

"Well I'm not."

"Okay. I'll do it all by myself. Just lend us your camera."

"No."

I stare at her. Hazel does her best to stare straight back.

"Hazel."

"*No*."

"Look Haze, it's embarrassing bringing this up, but if it weren't for me, you wouldn't even *have* a camera, remember? And it got stolen in the first place because you wouldn't go up the Eiffel Tower. And I rather nobly gave up *my* chance of going up the Eiffel Tower just to keep you company. And you were ever so grateful, right? And *I* said, that's what friends are for. To stick together."

"Oh Stevie," Hazel says despairingly.

"And yet now when *I* really need *you* . . ."

"Okay. I'll come with you. With the camera," says Hazel. Then she pauses. "But we still don't know where to go. I mean, these rats – they could be anywhere. I don't see how we're ever going to work it out." She sounds quite cheerful suddenly.

"I'll work it out if it's the last thing I do," I say determinedly.

Hazel droops again. And then she brightens.

"But how are we going to get away by ourselves? They'll be watching us like hawks. And we've only got till twelve o'clock."

"It's a free morning tomorrow. We can go anywhere we like!" I trill triumphantly.

I've forgotten to whisper. Mrs Wainwright suddenly opens her bedroom door along the corridor and peers out.

"Who's that shouting?" she sighs wearily. "Stephanie Day. I might have known. Haven't you caused enough

74

trouble for one day?"

I pause – and then start laughing. "Oh very good, Mrs Wainwright. Did you get that pun, Hazel? I'm causing enough trouble for one Day. Get it? I *am* a Day and . . ."

"And it's now getting on for night and you and Hazel are going straight back to your room after supper and you're staying there, do you hear? And tomorrow morning you're certainly not going to be trusted to go off by yourselves. You'd both better come round with me."

"Mrs Wainwright!" I think frantically. "I can see why you think we need to be punished – even though I swear it wasn't our fault, these gypsy girls truly did snatch Hazel's camera and then there really is this Mr Smoothie man – but anyway, I know you were all worried and so of course you want to punish us – but why punish *yourself*? Think how awful it would be for you to be stuck with us all morning! Think how noisy we are. Think how I'd be making silly jokes all the time and getting on your nerves. You must be getting really fed up with us by now. Think how lovely it would be for you to push off by yourself and see a bit of Paris in peace."

Hazel is holding her breath, looking terrified. Mrs Wainwright isn't at all the sort of teacher you can cheek. But she's also got a sense of humour . . . and thank goodness she suddenly smiles.

"You've got a point there, Stephanie," she says. "All right. You and Hazel can keep your free morning – so long as you stick with the others and behave yourselves. You've been naughty girls, giving us so much bother and worry – but I'm inclined to believe you about the camera. You can get a bit carried away at times, but I know you don't tell downright lies."

I smile back at her. She's not such a bad old stick after all. And I have a sudden brainwave.

"I've got a little present for you, Mrs Wainwright," I

say, and I dive back into our bedroom. I emerge with the enormously expensive English newspaper.

"I – I sort of came by this by accident today," I say. "Perhaps you'd like to relax with it after supper? It's got a bit bashed about and crumpled but it's still perfectly readable."

"That's very kind of you, Stephanie," she says. "What a very pleasant idea."

Supper proves to be a deeply suspect meaty stew – and no one can quite work out what the meat is. Elaine suggests that it's horse, and insists there are actually special horse-meat shops in Paris. Michelle is mad on ponies and immediately puts her fork down.

"Of course it's not horse," I say encouragingly. "These are *little* bits of animal body. What sort of animals are dirt cheap and in plentiful supply? Here, maybe it's rats."

Hazel puts her fork down too and groans. Elaine actually takes me seriously.

"It wouldn't be the first time Parisians have eaten rats," she says pompously. "Did you know, in the Paris siege they were so hungry they – "

"They prodded all the boring brainy people to death with their forks," I say, giving a demonstration. "And then they baked them and basted them and boiled them and had an immense feast, right?" I'm about to start a more serious attack but Mrs Wainwright's eye is on me and I subside.

Hazel and I still have to stay stuck in our room after supper while everyone else can go out and about – but it gives us time to try to solve this infuriating rat mystery.

Elaine's got a big map of Paris but although Hazel and I pore over it for hours we can't find a single Rat Street – or any monument or place remotely ratty either.

"I wonder if it's a pub?" I suggest. "You know, like we have The Bull or The Bear or The Ram. And they could

76

be meeting up under the pub sign."

"I don't think they have those sort of pubs in Paris," says Hazel. "It's all sort of bar-café places with tables outside – and they'd never call somewhere like that Les Rats. I mean, who'd go and eat and drink there, if it was called that?"

"Well, you come up with an idea then, if you keep sneering at all of mine."

"I don't know. I don't really want to know either. I still think we should keep out of it. Mrs Wainwright actually says she knows you don't tell lies, Stevie, so you don't have to fuss about that any more. Let's just forget about these stupid rats and that horrid man and – and enjoy ourselves."

But I can't forget it. I dream about rats all night long. They squeak and scrabble all around me, and try as I might I can't work out what they mean. When I wake up I find I'm sitting bolt upright in bed, my fists clenched, my heart pounding.

I thread my way through the beds and look out of the shuttered window. The sun's shining, dappling the newly washed street below me. Lots of people are already up and about, going to the early market along the road from us. One man's carrying a huge bunch of flowers. It looks as if he's raided those Botanical Gardens where we had our lunch! Those gardens . . .

I suddenly remember. They had a zoo there. Maybe you get rats in a zoo. You certainly get those great big Coypu things.

"I know where I want to go," I tell Hazel at breakfast. "The Botanical Gardens. Okay?"

Hazel looks surprised but relieved. "Okay," she says.

"You want to go to the Jardin des Plantes again?" says Elaine, frowning. "But we went there yesterday. What's the point of going there again?"

"I like it there," I say.

77

"Well, Michelle and I want to have a good explore all round the Latin Quarter, don't we – so I don't see how we can be in two places at once."

"The Latin Quarter! It's bad enough trying to make yourself understood in French."

"Oh ha ha. They don't *speak* Latin, idiot. It's all the stylish studenty bit. There's lots of famous cafés and some super shops," says Elaine.

Hazel looks tempted. "I do want to get some holiday presents, Stevie," she says wistfully.

"Well, we'll go to this zoo place first, and then maybe we'll go round a few shops," I say quickly – wondering when on earth I'm going to do my shopping for presents. If I've got any money left, that is. The Jardin des Plantes is right the other end of Paris from our hotel, so we'll have to spend more money on the Metro.

"It's a waste of time and money going back there, Stevie. I'm not going," says Elaine.

"Oh my heart bleeds," I say, gobbling down my baguette.

"Yes, but we've got to go round in groups of four or more. And we're your group," says Elaine. "You've got to go where your group wants, Stevie. And we want to go to the Boulevard St. Michel, don't we, Michelle? Your namesake, eh? And you'd like it there too, Hazel. So you'll just have to go along with us, Stevie."

"You lot can go where you want, I don't care," I say. "*I'm* going to the Botanical Gardens, so tough."

"You can't go on your own."

"I'll go in a group with Terry and them," I say, waving at Terry and his mates across the table. "Here Terry – can Haze and I tag along with you lot this morning?"

"Sure!"

"Hazel doesn't *want* to come with you," says Elaine furiously.

"Yes I do," says Hazel, but she sighs.

I give her hand a squeeze under the table . "Let's try really hard to find these rats, Haze – before twelve o'clock. But then afterwards, once we've got the photo, then I swear we'll go anywhere you like."

"We've got to be back here by one o'clock," says Hazel. "And if we're late Mrs Wainwright will explode."

"We're not going to be late, I promise. Now come on."

We have to line up in our groups after breakfast. Elaine and Michelle go off with two other girls. Hazel and I get together with Terry and all six of his mates.

"You're too big a group," says Mrs Wainwright. "You'll be too noisy and boisterous."

"Don't you worry, Mrs Wainwright. Us girls will keep them under control," I say.

Mrs Wainwright seems to have lost her sense of humour today. She just snorts – but she lets us go off together.

Terry and his mates haven't got any fixed plans for where they want to go, so I talk them into going to the zoo.

"It's where you wanted to go yesterday, right? It'll be great. And it's just over the river from the Bastille. You know, the prison that they seized in the Revolution." (I've been hastily skimming through Elaine's guide book.) They get quite carried away at the thought of the Bastille and its bloody history. If they knew a bit *more* about its history they'd know it was totally demolished and there's nothing to see at all in the square where it used to be . . . but I'll plead ignorance when the time comes.

It's good fun travelling on the Metro. It's crowded with French people going to work and they look a bit grim at first, but then these young buskers leap into our carriage. One sings, one plays a guitar, and the third does a little puppet show by turning his hand into a little head, inking in a face and wrapping a hankie round as a headscarf. The head speaks French, of course, but it's so cute we laugh even though we don't understand what it's saying.

The singing one comes round with an old hat and everyone drops in a few centimes.

"What a good idea," I say, when they jump out at the next station. "Here, Haze, have you got a hankie?" I try inking some eyes onto my hand with an old biro.

"I'm a good singer, I'm in a group at home," says one of Terry's mates.

"I can do handstands and acrobatics," says Terry. "Only there mightn't be enough room. We're all a bit jam-packed."

"If you lot start busking I shall *die* of embarrassment," says Hazel faintly.

She's in luck. We get to our Metro station before we've got our act properly sorted out. But it's still a good idea for the future . . .

The flowers are blooming in the Botanical Gardens but we don't pay them much heed. We make for the Menagerie and Hazel and I rush round the cages, while the boys take longer, mucking about and making odd animal noises.

"I don't like this zoo very much," says Hazel. "It's so old fashioned and cruel. Look at that poor old bear in that dirty pit. It's awful. What's the French for R.S.P.C.A.?"

"We can't think about the poor bear now, Haze. It's the rats we want." I tug the sleeve of a large French granny who's holding up a petite fille to wave at the monkey. "Excusez-moi, Madame, mais où sont les rats?"

"Les *rats*?" she says, pulling a face.

"Oui."

"Non! Pas ici." She shakes her head and laughs at the

idea.

"Isn't there a little corner pour les enfants? Avec les lapins? Et les – les cochons de Guinea? Et peut être les souris? Et les rats blancs?"

"Non," she says decidedly. She catches the eye of her grown-up daughter. "Les Anglais!" she says.

"Why you want see the rats?" says the daughter in hesitant English.

"I – I like rats. Very much," I say. "I really wanted to find some."

The daughter says something in French to her mother, who nods.

"We think there is a shop with lots of strange animals – possibly rats – down by the Seine, on the Right Bank."

"Great!" I say. "Come on, Hazel!"

Seven

"Hey, Stevie! Where are you off to?" Terry yells after me.

I hesitate. I wonder about telling him everything. If Terry was just by himself it would be easy enough. He'd maybe even *believe* me about Mr Smoothie – not like some people I could mention. But Terry's not by himself. He's got all his mates – and they'd never take any of it seriously. They wouldn't help search for these mysterious rats. They'd just muck about and be stupid. Look at them now, all pretending to be monkeys, leaping about bow-legged and scratching themselves in rude places. The real monkeys peer at them indifferently through the bars of their cages. Garçons will be garçons.

"Haze and I are going to this shop now, Terry," I say quickly. "We'll see you later."

"Which shop? We'll come too."

"You don't want to go *shopping*," I say.

"I didn't think you would either, Stevie," says Terry. "Come on, come to the Bastille with us. And then we could go to the Pompidou Centre – we went past it in the coach yesterday. It's this weird modern building a bit like a boat with funnels and there are all these glass lifts on the outside and escalators all over the place – we couldn't half have fun."

I know we could. There's part of me that would love to forget all about this Wild Rat Chase and go off with

Terry. I know that's what Hazel wants too – although she doesn't look too keen on the glass lift idea. But I do so want to sort out this rat thing, and prove Mr Smoothie is a crook. It's as if I've got this awful itch and it won't go away no matter how much I scratch.

"Sorry Terry. We really want to push off on our own now," I say.

He shrugs. "Suit yourself then," he says huffily.

"Maybe we'll be able to meet up at this Pompidou place later," I suggest.

"Don't bother about it. There's lots of the others going there. Lucy and some of her friends," says Terry.

"Oh." I can't think of anything else to say.

We all cross over the Pont Sully in silence. Then Terry and his mates go up the Boulevard to the Bastille. Hazel and I walk along the river bank.

"Stevie?" says Hazel.

"Mm?"

"I don't think he was really meeting up with Lucy. He was just saying that to get at you," she says.

"I don't care if he meets up with Lucy and *marries* her," I say fiercely. "It's a matter of supreme indifference to me, Hazel."

"Yes Stevie," says Hazel.

We plod on in silence.

"I just want to track down these rats. And then hide until twelve and take the photo, right?" I say eventually.

"Right," says Hazel, but she sounds doubtful.

I'm beginning to feel doubtful myself. But maybe I'll find a whole cage of rats at this shop. A high cage, so that they can meet *under* it. That *is* what he said, I'm sure of it.

We find the shop at last, after a long treck – and the woman was right, there are heaps of strange animals in cages. A duck pokes its beak through the cage and nearly frightens Hazel to death. Chickens cluck frantically. A rooster crows. Rabbits huddle into their fur, their ears flat.

"They're frightened, poor little things. And there're far too many in their cage," says Hazel.

"No wonder they're frightened – look at those horrible ferretty things in the cage right next to them. It's like us living in the next door room to a lot of homicidal maniacs with double-barrelled shotguns," I say.

"Stevie – you don't think those men might have guns?" Hazel says worriedly, looking over her shoulder. "Because if we jump out and take a photo then what happens if they spot us? It might panic them. They might shoot first and then . . . well, it would be too late for us, wouldn't it?"

"Imagine our funerals," I say, reaching into the rabbit cage and stroking their soft fur. "We could have a joint one – and Mrs Wainwright and Mr Mason and Ms Mosely would be dressed all in black – your lover-boy would have to dye one of his white teeshirts for the occasion – and then when it was all over and our families have driven away in their funeral cars all three teachers would linger in the graveyard, feeling so guilty. Mr Mason and Ms Mosely might eventually wander off hand in hand under the yew trees but Mrs Wainwright would prostrate herself on our joint graves and wail a lament –"

"Do shut up, Stevie. It's not a joke, you know. We really could get shot," says Hazel. "Do let's get away from this awful animal shop. Those ferrets are looking at me. I'm sure they could get their heads through those bars."

"There are some white mice, look! Over at the back. Oh Haze, there's got to be rats too."

I peer into each and every cage – but I can't find a single rat anywhere. An old man assistant is frowning at me severely by this time.

"Avez-vous des rats, Monsieur?" I ask.

"Non," he says.

"Êtes-vous absolutement sure?" I ask, unwilling to give up.

"Stevie! He said no. *Do* come away. There's a dead chicken in the corner of that cage and it's making me feel ill," says Hazel.

"Maybe it's not a pet. Maybe it's lunch for one of the other animals," I say. "Boa constrictors like chicken, don't they? And r-a-b-b-i-t. Although I don't need to spell it, these are little French rabbits, aren't they? So they won't speak English. Hey, do snakes eat rats? Could they be dead rats? Excusez moi, Monsieur, mais avez-vous des rats morts?"

He is making it plain that he doesn't have a rat on the entire premises, dead or alive. Not even a stuffed rat. Not even a little toy rubber rat . . .

"It mightn't be real rats!" I say excitedly to Hazel. "They could be toy ones, couldn't they?"

"You don't get toy rats," says Hazel.

"Yes, you do! Those rubber things. You know, the black wobbly sort. I bought a giant spider once to frighten Carla – "

"*That* sort," says Hazel.

"So come on – let's find a toy shop."

"Stevie. This is stupid. Those men aren't going to be meeting in a toy shop. Don't be so silly."

"I think it's a very sensible place to meet up – because it's so unlikely. You're hardly likely to bump into the French drugs squad in the middle of a toy shop."

"But there must be hundreds of toy shops in Paris. We can't go and search them all for rubber rats. And it's half past ten already. They're meeting up at twelve, according to you. If it really was midi."

"I *think* it was," I say, sighing – because Hazel's made me see this is all a bit pointless. I'm making all these wild guesses instead of thinking logically. So. I try logic.

85

"Let's suppose they really are meeting up under some sort of rats. At twelve o'clock today. Right? And we don't think they're wild rats, because they wouldn't stay in the same place. And they can't be caged rats either, because we can't find any. So perhaps they're toy rats. Okay? Well, suppose they are meeting up in a toy shop. Or a toy department, say? Yes! That would be bigger, more anonymous, wouldn't it? And it would probably be somewhere quite central. They don't want to go chasing right across Paris, do they? They met up in *Smiths* in the Rue de Rivoli. That's just up that street there. So what's the nearest big department store?"

We stare along the road. And see the big sign of *Samaritaine*.

"Before our very eyes," I say. "Come on, Haze." She still looks a bit fed up. "We'll look for some toy rats, right? But we can also have a look round the whole shop, maybe buy some holiday presents, just have a good time, yes?"

"Yes!" says Hazel fervently.

Samaritaine has got an incredible toy department. For a minute or two we wander round dazed, shaking hands with huge toy monkeys and stroking sleek toy tigers.

"It makes me wish I was little again. I'd love to take Poppy here," I say, making a tiger growl at Hazel.

"Look at the prices!" Hazel says. "Do put it back, Stevie, you'll upset all the display. Oh, look at those *dolls*."

She goes into raptures over some big baby dolls with cases full of dinky little clothes. There's one that cries when you pull a string. It sounds just like my little stepbrother Benjamin. I twang his string and give his little plastic nose a tweak.

"Stop that row, little baby, I can't hear myself think," I say. "Now, rats. Où sont les petits rubber rats?"

We stop playing with the toys and start searching.

"Hey! What's French for eureka!" I cry, because right at the end of one counter I spot a little basket full of tiny wobbly rubber animals. It's like a bowl of black and brown and green jelly. There's spiders, octopus, prehistoric monsters, snakes . . . I scoop up great handfuls, searching for a ratty tail amongst all the claws and paws and tentacles.

"Ugh," says Hazel, and when I wriggle an octopus in her face she starts shrieking.

"Sh, Haze! That assistant's looking at you," I say primly.

There isn't a rat in sight. It's terribly disappointing. But I do find a little black rubber bat, the sort that fits on the end of a finger. I try it on and flap its wings.

"Isn't it sweet? I'm going to buy it for Poppy. It can be a little friend for her big toy bat Boris. It's only three francs, great. I wonder if Carla would like one too? She didn't seem to appreciate that spider I bought her. And I don't suppose Laura would really care for one either. But there's my Dad. I could get him a big snake. Yeah, highly appropriate."

"Stevie! You can't possibly give your Dad a rubber snake! What about a scarf? That's what I'm going to get for my Mum or my Nan. Can we go and find the scarves next?"

I buy the little bat for Poppy and then go down to the ground floor with Hazel to look for boring old scarves. It seems an awful waste of time. It's eleven o'clock now. I'd really like to dash off to some other department store, see if they stock toy rats – but I can see that Hazel's had it up to here with rats. I suppose it's only fair if we have a wander round *Samaritaine*. The world won't come to an end just because I haven't solved the great rat mystery. My detective friend Cathy has often drummed it into me that you can't hope to solve all your cases. You've got to let some of them go. You can't keep on

87

searching for an answer when you know you haven't a clue. You'd go crazy. And maybe I'm crazy enough already.

So I help Hazel choose a chiffon scarf for her Mum and a lacy hankie for her Nan with *Je t'aime* embroidered in one corner.

"Pity they don't do men's hankies with *Je te deteste* embroidered on them," I say. "No, there's nothing here that'll do for any of my lot. Laura's not really the scarf sort."

We move on to the cosmetic counters. I fancy buying Laura a bottle of French perfume and Hazel happily tries them out for me on her wrists – but when we see the prices we both reel. I settle for a cake of French soap instead.

"I think it smells just as nice," I say. "Nicer, in fact. What did you have to put all that stuff on for, Haze? You don't half pong."

"I think it smells lovely," says Hazel. "Do you think Mr Mason likes perfume on a woman, Stevie?"

"I think he'll keel right over if you waft past him," I say. "I'll get bath oil for Cathy – she likes a good long soak after a long day on duty. Now what about Carla? She asked for earrings or a teeshirt but I'm not going to have enough money left."

"What about a special French shampoo? Your sister's got such lovely hair," says Hazel, running her fingers through her own skimpy locks and sighing.

"Good idea. Something for the famous Carla curls," I say.

There's a whole stand of elaborate hair slides and hairbands. I have great fun trying some of them on, though my own hair is in its usual schoolboy stubble style.

"Which shall it be? The diamanté butterfly? Or the plastic pink piglets?"

Hazel advises a pair of plain gilt slides, curved so that they look like the letter C. I think they're a bit boring but I let myself be persuaded.

"And now there's just your Dad," says Hazel.

"Well, I don't think hair slides are quite his scene."

"Well, what is?"

"*I* don't know."

"Stevie, he's your Dad."

Hazel doesn't have a father herself and therefore thinks that all fathers are something special – even mine.

"What are his hobbies, eh?"

"He doesn't really have any hobbies. When he's not working or bossing people about he just sits around with his head in a book."

"There! We'll get him a book. A French book. He can speak French, can't he?"

"I suppose so. He's always going on about how brainy he is and how we'll have to work much much harder if we ever want to do as well as him. A book will be too expensive though."

"A paperback?"

But when we start browsing round the book department we find most French books are paperbacks – and all of them horrifically expensive.

"It's probably because they're all quite big. What about those little books on that stand over there? Those little art books."

"He quite likes art. Yeah, that looks the sort of boring old stuff he likes. Old Masters. I like modern Art. All bright splashy colours. I mean, this seventeenth century stuff – it's just one big yawn – "

And then I stop – and stare. I'm looking at a painting by some bloke called Poussin. It's obviously of some sort of plague, because there are dead bodies everywhere. It's strange, it looks quite pretty at first glance, all rose and peach and blue and gold, so that it's like a thump in the stomach when you see all these people are actually shrieking and dying, though in a very sedate statuesque sort of way. And when I screw my eyes up and look at the small reproduction really carefully I see something else. *Rats*! There are several of them, scurrying down the street.

I look at the bottom of the painting. It says it's in the Louvre museum. The Louvre museum in Paris.

"I've got it!" I squeal. "That's where they're meeting. And I tell you what. They could easily shove a little drugs package behind the painting – so it would be under the rats! Come on, Hazel – we've got to go to the Louvre, to find this Poussin painting. Come on." I stick the little book back in its stand – it's still too expensive for my Dad – grab Hazel's hand, and pull.

"But it's too late. It's nearly half past eleven."

"Then we'd better run."

"Run round Paris?"

But we're in luck. Because guess which huge building is almost next door to *Samaritaine*? You've got it. The Louvre.

But it's not quite that simple. It takes us a long while to find the way in, and then it takes even longer to weave our way through the crowds. We have to pay, which is pretty sick-making – and we waste time queuing up for our ticket. I keep looking at the time and sighing impatiently.

"You are very keen to see the paintings, mademoiselle?" says this twinkly-eyed fat man behind me.

"Yes, very," I say. "Er . . . do you know the galleries well, Monsieur? You don't happen to know where the seventeenth century paintings are, do you?"

His eyebrows go up. He smiles at me approvingly.

"The seventeenth century!" he says. "Such taste!" His sexy French accent makes it difficult to tell if he's taking

90

the mick or not. If he were thirty years younger and several stone lighter I might quite fancy him. We're getting on like a house on fire. Hazel is staring at us open-mouthed.

"Would it be the Italian seventeenth century – or the French?"

"Oh, the French – I think," I say. "Poussin is French, isn't he?"

"Indeed yes. And you admire the works of Poussin, Mademoiselle? Well, well! When one is so young one does not usually admire the works of the great classical period."

He's practically patting me on the head. He gives me detailed instructions on how to find all these Poussin paintings in the Grande Galerie on the first floor. I buy two tickets at the desk – I suppose it's only fair I fork out for Hazel, although it means I've hardly any money left at all – and then I turn round to say a quick merci and au revoir.

I'm in the middle of my thanks when I spot a very familiar figure coming out of the first gallery. There can't be two powder blue trouser suits in Paris. Especially that size.

Mrs Wainwright's mouth drops open as she spots Hazel and me. I suppose it isn't quite our usual venue.

"Hello girls!" she says, coming over to us. "I can't quite believe my eyes. I had no idea you wanted to come to the Louvre."

"Ah well. We have hidden depths," I say uneasily.

"Yes, Stephanie. You generally keep your cultural depths exceptionally well hidden," says Mrs Wainwright. "But there you are – we could have accompanied each other perfectly amicably this morning after all."

"Well. I don't know about that. We like to have a very *quick* look, don't we, Haze? We'd actually better be going – we don't want to be late back for lunch, do we?"

Mrs Wainwright shakes her head slightly, as if she can't quite take in what I'm saying.

"Excuse me, Madame." It's my twinkly-eyed fat Monsieur, addressing Mrs Wainwright. "Are these delightful young ladies in your care? I'm very impressed by their scholarly interest in art. The young lady with the short hair tells me she is particularly interested in the great French classical period of the seventeenth century."

"She said that?" says Mrs Wainwright weakly.

"Well. We're going to look at the Poussin paintings, aren't we, Hazel?" I say. "Must dash. Goodbye Mrs Wainwright. Au revoir encore, Monsieur."

He laughs delightedly and takes off his hat to me. Mrs Wainwright sways on her feet, utterly staggered. Hazel and I dash off, and the moment we're out of sight we fall about laughing.

"Her face!" we groan, clutching at each other.

But then I catch sight of the time and sober up.

"Come on, Haze. It's getting on for twelve!"

We charge up the stairs and along the endless galleries, dodging little flocks of American and Japanese tourists obediently marching from masterpiece to masterpiece. An assistant frowns and shakes his finger at us, saying something in French which is probably stop running. We don't hang about long enough to find out. We charge onwards, and at last spot some paintings of rather stiff rosy-cheeked people in togas looking as if they're playing a game of statues.

"That looks like Poussin," I say – and blow me, it is! Maybe I've got a real flair for this Art History lark. Maybe when I'm a very famous detective in the Metropolitan Police I can also give the odd lecture at the National Gallery in my spare time.

"I can't see any rats," says Hazel.

"It was a painting of the Plague," I say, sidling along. "Oh no, don't say it's not here."

I hurry from Poussin to Poussin – and then I spot it! I see the dead woman, the dead baby, the poor terrified crying child, the agonized people – *and the rats*!

"There they are! Oh Haze! We've found them!"

"If they're the right rats," says Hazel.

"They've got to be. And it's three minutes to twelve."

"Oh help!" Hazel looks round nervously. There's no sign of Mr Smoothie, Mr Scruffy, or the silly girlfriend. "Have you got your camera at the ready, Haze? I wonder where we can lurk? Up the gallery a bit, I suppose. Here, I wonder if the package could already be behind the painting? Hidden away, under the rats? Maybe Mr Scruffy or someone has already hidden it there! Shall I take a peek?"

"No, Stevie!"

But I've got to find out. I take another quick look round. There's no one looking my way. The attendant is sitting back on his chair, yawning.

"*Stevie*!" Hazel hisses.

I take no notice. I approach the painting. There's a very large rat on the left. So I take hold of the ornate gold frame on the left of the painting and very very carefully try to prise it a fraction from the wall, to see if there's anything hidden behind. But as I prise, there's a sudden awful ringing of an alarm – and someone suddenly seizes hold of me!

Eight

I'm surrounded by shouting gesticulating people – and I can't understand a word any of them are saying. The attendant has got hold of me so tightly I can hardly draw breath. The alarm keeps ringing and ringing so I can't even think straight. I see someone's wristwatch – it's spot on midi, twelve o'clock exactly. Only they won't come within a mile of this gallery now, when there's all this uproar.

They've got hold of Hazel too, which is so unfair because *I* was the one who touched the painting and set off the alarm, poor old Hazel didn't do a thing. They're shouting at her too, and she shakes her head desperately and says "I'm sorry, I don't understand, please, we didn't mean to do anything bad." But they go on shouting at her and I just can't stand it.

"Leave her alone, you great bullies! She's got nothing to do with this! Let her go. And stop shouting at her, shouting won't get you anywhere," I yell, though I'm certainly shouting myself.

The American and Japanese tourists are trying to flock round us, gawping as if we're some extraordinary live exhibit. They get shouted at too, but they take no notice. My attendant shouts something else and then starts pulling at me. I'm yanked along the gallery and then shoved into a little side room. Hazel is pulled after me.

"Oh Stevie," she says, starting to cry.

"Don't cry, Haze. It's all right. They'll calm down soon and see it's all a silly mistake. They can't *do* anything to us. We're only children," I gabble as reassuringly as I can – but I can't quite reassure myself, let alone Hazel.

I know it's mad but I can't help thinking about that terrible Conciergerie place where they kept the women and children locked up. They can't lock us up, we haven't even done anything – and even if they do, they certainly aren't going to drag us off to the Guillotine. Although France still has the odd rusty Guillotine or two, doesn't it? But not for kids who've simply touched a painting in a gallery, for goodness sake . . .

They're shouting at me again and it's no use. I can't seem to understand any French at all. I don't think I'd twig what they were yelling if they were speaking ordinary English. It's all too scary all of a sudden. And what's going to happen next? I suppose they'll call for the police. And they'll cart us off to the police station and there'll be more shouted questions . . .

I know one thing, we're never going to get back to the hotel in time for lunch. I think with sudden extraordinary yearning of Mrs Wainwright. If I saw her now I'd fling my arms round her and cry on that capacious powder blue bosom.

"Mrs Wainwright!" I cry. "Peut-être elle est dans le Louvre still. She's our teacher. Our professeur. Our professeutte? We're her élèves, don't you see? Nous sommes just *kids*. I was just mucking about. I just wanted to look behind the painting, what it was like. Oh help. Doesn't anyone parlez Anglais?"

The door opens and someone who's obviously a senior security man walks in briskly. His face is stern – but when he sees us two he shakes his head and then bursts out laughing. He says something rapidly in French and they answer. He shakes his head again.

"So, mesdemoiselles, you are both dangerous art thieves, yes?" he says.

"No! My friend was just looking at the painting," Hazel sobs.

But I can see he's not serious.

"I was just being silly. I know I shouldn't have touched the painting. I'm sorry," I say meekly. "Our schoolteacher might still be in the building. She'll vouch for us. She'll be absolutely livid, of course, but she'll swear that we're not *thieves*."

"I think maybe I can see that too," he says. "Although of course *I* am . . . absolutely livid. You naughty girls have upset all my staff and caused a major incident. So what are we going to do with you, hmm?"

"Give us a severe telling off – and then let us go? We're supposed to be back at our hotel by one o'clock for our lunch," I say.

He smiles. "That sounds reasonable," he says. "We can't have you missing out on your lunch. But first, the severe telling off."

He's not smiling now. He gives us this serious lecture about precious paintings and security and how tiresome it is when idiotic children disrupt the system – and Haze and I nod and murmur apologies. And then at last he shakes us both by the hand and lets us go.

When we emerge from the room there's still a few stray tourists staring goggle-eyed. I wave at them jauntily and ask if they want the autographs of two daring art thieves.

"Shut *up*, Stevie," says Hazel.

She scarcely says another word to me on the Metro back to our hotel. I think she might have had enough of me for the moment.

I'm a bit fed up with me myself. If I hadn't messed about with the flipping Poussin painting we could maybe

96

have seen the famous meeting at midi, taken a quick photo, and then used it as undeniable evidence. But now I've blown it. They'll meet up another day, in another place – and I won't ever have a chance of catching them in the act.

The great rat race is over. I've tripped us up well before the finishing line.

I don't cheer up when we get back to the hotel, even though we're in plenty of time. Terry and his mates are ten minutes late. Lucy and Terry are hand in hand and smirking at each other. They don't even get told off for being late, because Mr Mason and Ms Mosely are also hand in hand and not in the mood for fierce confrontations. Mrs Wainwright doesn't tell them off – because she's not here. *Mrs Wainwright* is late back. We're all halfway through our rather suspect fish and frites when she comes rushing into the dining room, scarlet in the face.

Ms Mosely has a little word, obviously wondering if something dramatic has happened to make her late. But Mrs Wainwright doesn't look as if she's been mugged on the Metro or run over by an autobus. She looks positively glowing, eyes all twinkly. Like my fat man in the Louvre.

But this newfound mellowness doesn't last and when we all start trading flavours of our Neapolitan ice-cream puddings – I like chocolate, Hazel likes the strawberry and Michelle at the other end of the table only likes vanilla – she gets irritated.

"Will you kindly *stop* distributing ice-cream all round the table. Now. The coach will be here at two thirty and I want you all to be lined up and waiting outside the hotel, do you understand? We're going to the Cluny Museum this afternoon. And then when we come back you can all get started on your projects."

I groan. I've had enough of museums for one day.

And upstairs in our bedroom Elaine the Pain starts burbling on about this Cluny Museum and it doesn't sound a bundle of laughs. It's all devoted to the Middle Ages and sounds one big yawn.

I do yawn, ostentatiously, while Elaine spouts from her boring old guide book. I switch off while she witters on about tapestries and statues and jewellery, and then she starts on about these two churches we're going to as well, just to make it a truly jolly little jaunt. St. Séverin and St. Julien le Pauvre.

"Never mind old Julien. I'm Stevie le Pauvre," I say, digging deep into my purse. "I've got hardly any money left, look. It's going to be tough if we have to fork out for this museum. I shall just have to lurk outside and peer through the windows. Unless I try my hand at a bit of busking."

"You dare," says Hazel.

Elaine is still droning ever onwards; about all these ancient streets round about. I actually start listening when she goes on about this old School of Medicine and the medical treatments in the Middle Ages. Did you know that if you boil 300 slugs and beat them up nicely with olive oil and honey the resulting goo makes your hair grow a treat? I'll recommend this method to my Dad when I go home.

Then Elaine reads out some even more bizarre treatments involving mice droppings, dog excrement and chopped kittens. I'm actually enthralled, although I wouldn't admit it for anything, but Hazel and Michelle are groaning and making being-sick noises.

"Do shut *up*, Elaine," says Hazel.

"This whole street has got the most extraordinary history," Elaine burbles on. "And it didn't use to be called the Rue de l'Hotel Colbert at all. It used to be called the – "

"We're not the slightest bit interested in what it used

to be called," I say, and I leap across the bed and snatch the guidebook from her hand.

I hold it at the open window, threatening to throw it out, and Elaine grabs hold of me, and then Hazel and Michelle start joining in too, hitting at us with their pillows, and we all end up in a yelling shrieking heap.

"Really girls!" says Mrs Wainwright, bursting in on us.

We think for a moment she's going to get ferociously angry, as per usual – but then she raises one eyebrow at me in sardonic fashion.

"What's the reason for all this hysterical excitement, Stephanie? Is it because you're going to another museum? I'm afraid the Middle Ages is a little early for your taste – but if you have an eye for the classical then you will delight in the ruins of the Roman baths still visible at Cluny."

"Oh, of course I'll delight in them, Mrs Wainwright," I say, extracting myself from the other three with difficulty.

In actual fact Cluny turns out to be a quite interesting old house, and it's not terribly big, which is a major advantage in a museum. And it doesn't really look much like a museum either, even though they can't help having some things in glass display cases. Some of the galleries are arranged like real medieval rooms, with all the right furniture. If Terry and I were on speaking terms we could maybe have a game or two. He's standing quite near me and I turn round casually to see what he's looking at. Oh. He's looking at Lucy.

I turn back and stare intently at the glass-topped trestle table right in front of me as if it's the most fascinating thing in the whole world. There's a picture of a poor little mangy lion, chained up to a tree. It's biting at its chain like mad but it doesn't look as if it's got a hope of gnawing through. There's a little grey rat beside its clawed foot and it's biting at the chain too – a little grey *rat*! And it's on the table. So you could put something underneath the table. Oh no! Maybe this was the meeting place, not the Louvre at all.

I feel tentatively under the table, the rough wood scratching my hand. You could easily attach a package and walk on – and then someone else could come into the room and remove it. At twelve o'clock. I look at my watch foolishly, although I know perfectly well it's three o'clock in the afternoon.

I go up to the attendant sitting on her chair in the corner.

"Excusez-moi, Madame, mais est-ce museum ouvert à douze heures? I know you close for lunch – pour déjeuner – mais vous êtes ouvert à douze heures?" I point to it on my watch.

She laughs. "Ouvert? Mais oui. A midi – pas à minuit."

"Pas à quoi?" I say, my ears suddenly tingling.

"Minuit." she laughs again, to show me she's joking.

I'm the joker. Why didn't I think. Minuit! The French way of saying twelve midnight. *That's* what Mr Smoothie said. It wasn't Mimi and it wasn't midi either. It was minuit. I learnt the word in French classes but I always pronounced it minn-wee. The French say it in a much quicker blurrier sort of way, so you don't really hear the "n" at all. Minuit.

Now I come to think of it, whoever heard of some shady sinister meeting taking place at midday? Of course it's midnight. Which means I'm still in with a chance!

So is this where they're meeting? In the Cluny Museum at midnight, under the little painted rat on this table. No. Somehow that's not quite logical. To start with, the security in the museum must be massive. There's all their medieval treasures. They'll all be wired up like the Poussin picture. And anyway, it would be a

100

pointless risk, breaking into the museum when there's probably lots of security men patrolling – and if they *did* manage it, they wouldn't need to fiddle about handing the package over at the ratty table, surely to goodness?

So I'm on the wrong track again. I still don't know where these rats are. I give a despairing sigh.

"What's up with you, Stevie?" says Terry, standing right beside me.

There's an infuriating gleam in his eyes.

"Nothing at all," I say, and I turn my heel and stalk off.

"Hey, hang about. I've got a bone to pick with you. We went to the Bastille like you suggested – and there's nothing there! Just a lot of traffic rushing about!"

"Really?" I say, as if I'm not very interested. "Oh well, never mind, Terry. I daresay you had quite a good morning even if you did run short on historic sites."

Terry grins. "Look Stevie, Lucy and me, well – "

Lucy comes simpering over to us.

"Did you call me, Terry?" she says, and she tucks her hand in his arm.

She's wearing the angora top again. Terry's nose is already twitching.

I march off to find Hazel and the others. I hear sneezing behind me. I smile.

Hazel's in raptures over some tapestries upstairs of a lady and her unicorn.

"I'm going to get more postcards of the tapestries. I'm going to do my project on them," she says happily.

Oh God. I'd forgotten. We're all supposed to do a special project on something French today and then hand them in during our evening meal. It's supposed to keep us nicely quiet between six and half past seven. Out of the way. While Mrs Wainwright and Mr Mason and Ms Mosely sneak off to the bar next door and sip the odd aperitif or two.

"What on earth can I do for my project then?" I say.

Mrs Wainwright is nearby. She turns and smiles at me.

"Oh Stephanie! Surely you'll choose the works of Poussin?"

It's game set and match to Mrs Wainwright – and she knows it.

"I think maybe I've had a bit much of Poussin for one day," I say. "I'll think up some other topic."

The Cluny Museum has got lots of quite interesting stuff if you're actually in the mood for museums. It's not all fearfully ornate and holy and precious. There's a medieval man's shoe for instance, that is fascinating, tapering into an enormously long point.

"They obviously had entirely different feet in those days," I say. "Or maybe they didn't have scissors so they couldn't cut their toenails. And the nail on the big toe would grow and grow and so the shoe had to be specially made to fit. Very useful if you met up with a dangerous foe actually. You could just whip off your shoe and stab him in the shins with your toenail."

Somehow I don't quite think I can stretch the topic of medieval men's footwear to two sides of file paper, Mrs Wainwright's stated minimum.

When we get back to the hotel Hazel and Michelle and Elaine the Pain start scribbling almost straight away. Hazel's doing the Lady and Unicorn tapestries, Michelle's writing about the jewellery and Elaine the Pain's embarking on a complete *book* on medieval monastery life, sigh shudder shriek.

So what am I going to do?

I ask this question. Several times. The others groan.

"I don't care what you do, Stevie, but I wish you'd stop going on about it," says Hazel.

"What are you really interested in?" says Michelle, trying to be helpful.

"Rats," I say.

Michelle looks taken aback.

"Rats?" she says uncertainly.

"Take no notice of her," says Hazel.

Elaine looks up from her monk project. She's already written a page and a half.

"Why don't you write about the *Rue des Rats*?" she says.

For a moment I don't think I've heard her properly.

"The *Rue des Rats*?" I say, very slowly.

"Mm."

"There isn't a Rue des Rats. Not in Paris," I say.

"Yes there is," says Elaine. She's writing as she speaks. It's not fair, she can even be brainy on automatic pilot.

"There *isn't*. I looked it up on your street map. There is not a single Rue des Rats."

"Not now. I *told* you. Well, I was about to tell you before you interrupted me. The Rue de l'Hotel Colbert used to be called the Rue des Rats. It's got all these interesting old buildings in it, including the old Faculty of Medicine. You were interested in that. The place where they boiled the slugs and – "

But I'm not a bit interested in the slugs now. It's the rats, the rats, the Rue des Rats.

"Are you sure it used to be called the Rue des Rats?" I say.

"Yes. It says in my guide book. There were once a lot of rats there – only it's actually a corruption of the word Arras. But the name of the street is carved into the stone wall. You can still see it."

"So someone could meet under the sign – under the rats!" I say, and I leap up.

Elaine ducks nervously as I approach.

But I throw my arms round her and hug her enthusiastically.

"My friend! My marvellous mine of information! I will

never never never call you Elaine the Pain again. From now on you are Elaine the *Brain*!!"

Nine

"Goodnight girls," says Mrs Wainwright. "Sleep tight. And not too much giggling and gossiping tonight, do you hear me?"

"Yes, Mrs Wainwright," we chorus.

She catches my eye.

"Stephanie! You look as if butter wouldn't melt in your mouth," she says, and she actually laughs. "So what are you up to, mm?"

"Nothing, Mrs Wainwright," I say, as innocently as possible.

"If that's true, then I'm a Dutchman," says Mrs Wainwright. She looks down at herself. "I don't see any clogs, do you?"

Actually she's not even in her usual sturdy lace-ups. Or her powder blue trouser suit for that matter. She's in nifty little patent heels and a floral frock that makes her look almost girlish. And she's acting girlish too, larking about with us like this.

Still, I haven't got time to suss out the reason for Mrs Wainwright's amazing change of character. I've got far more important things on my mind.

As soon as she's out the door I stop hugging the bedclothes up to my chin. I leap out of bed, fully dressed except for my shoes and jacket.

"Come on, Hazel," I say.

Hazel groans desperately but obeys.

"Will you tell us what on earth you two are up to?" Elaine asks, for the fifty seventh time.

"You can't go out now. It's half past *ten*," says Michelle.

"Oh dear. Let's hope we're not turned into pumpkins," I say, stepping into my shoes.

"Stevie! If the teachers catch you and Hazel - "

Hazel moans.

"They *won't*," I say very firmly.

"But anyway, it's not safe, wandering round Paris by yourselves after dark."

"We'll be okay."

"But *why* – ?"

"We want to take a special photograph," I say. "Got the camera safe, Haze? Come on, then."

We creep out of the bedroom, closing the door on Elaine and Michelle's whispered questions. There's a night porter at the reception desk, but he's got his ear glued to some sporting event on his transistor radio and he doesn't blink when we scoot across the hallway and out the front door.

"How are we ever going to get back in?" Hazel asks. "I'm sure they lock the door some time."

"No they won't. Or if they do, we'll have to knock. Oh *Hazel*. Don't keep making up more problems," I snap irritably, because I don't know how we're going to get back in either.

"I don't have to make them up. They occur all by themselves," says Hazel miserably. "Oh Stevie, what are we *doing*? We don't even know how to get to this *Rue des Rats* place. And it's dark and it is dangerous and – "

"Don't worry, Hazel. I'll look after you."

She gives me a withering look.

"No, really. I've got it all worked out. We'll get the Metro. The only problem is, I'm not sure I've got enough cash. You have got your purse with you, haven't you?"

Hazel sighs again.

"Cheer up. You ought to be excited. I mean, this is an incredible adventure. Here we are, at night in a foreign city, on the trail of desperate drug-dealers or whatever – I don't think even my friend Cathy has been involved in something as big as this."

"I wish I wasn't involved," Hazel sniffs. "And I think we're lost already. I don't remember this street."

"This is a quick way to the Metro station," I say hopefully. "I chose it because – because it's all light and bright with lots of cafés and restaurants. So it's safe. Right?"

Thank goodness, after a rather long walk and several further streets, I spot the familiar Metro sign with its droopy art nouveau lettering. And that's not all I spot! I stare into a very flash looking café, transfixed.

"Look who's there!" I whisper to Hazel.

"Mr Smoothie?" she says, looking terrified.

"No! Look. At that corner table at the back, see."

Hazel looks. Hazel sees for herself.

"*Gosh*!"

It's Mrs Wainwright. But she's not alone. She's smiling straight into the twinkly eyes of my fat man from the Louvre! They've got two glasses and a bottle of wine on their table. He's pouring her a glass – and then they drink to each other, clinking glasses. He's saying something – and Mrs Wainwright giggles girlishly.

"But she's *Mrs* Wainwright," says Hazel.

"Oh come on. Remember the way Mr Wainwright was oggling at Ms Mosely when we were getting on the coach back in England. Maybe she's entitled to a little fun," I say. Then I pause. "Of course, we could always take a little snap of them now – and then if Mrs Wainwright is furiously angry with me in the future I could just flash it in front of her nose? I'm *joking*,

107

Hazel."

We leave the lovebirds and go to the Metro. The station itself is a bit scary, with quite a few drunks and creepy-looking blokes lurking in corners. One of them approaches Hazel and starts making kiss-kiss noises at her. I say something very rude indeed. I'm not sure he understands that sort of English but he seems to get the message all the same. He shuffles off, mumbling similar suggestions in colloquial French.

It's a relief when the train comes at last. I'm more worried than I let on, because after a bit we've got to change to a different line so we can cross the river. But more by luck than judgement we get off one train, change onto another and arrive at the St. Michel Metro station on the Left Bank with no problems at all – and it's still only ten past eleven, so we're in plenty of time.

It's okay at first because the Boulevard St Michel is packed with people enjoying an evening out, and everywhere's brightly lit. It's a bit more worrying when we have to turn along the Rue St Severin and the Rue St Julien le Pauvre, the two churches we visited after the Cluny. But there's still the odd restaurant around, and quite a few couples. It's a lot more scary when we're actually in the Rue de l'Hotel Colbert. It's very dark and very deserted.

"Oh Stevie," Hazel whispers, and she clutches my arm.

"We've got here, Haze! Cheer up! We've done the hardest part already. Now we've just got to find this old street sign of the Rue des Rats and then we can select our hiding place and – and Bob's your Uncle."

"I've got an Uncle Bob actually," says Hazel.

"There you are then. That's a good omen," I say breezily.

"He had a heart attack last month," says Hazel.

My own heart is hammering away like mad, though

I'm doing my best to put on a brave front for Hazel's sake. Somehow it was all a bit of a game before, even though I thought I was deadly serious. Now we're actually here in the Rue des Rats in the dark I can't help panicking a bit. What if the drug dealers arrive early for the rendez-vous, spot us – and realize what we're up to?

No, I *can't* play the what-if game. I've got to keep my mind clear and get us organized.

We've got to find this old street sign. Then we'll know exactly where they're meeting. It's no use our lurking down one end of the street if they're meeting up at the other. The sign's meant to be scratched on an old wall. But all the walls in this street look old – so far as you can tell in the dark.

Why didn't I bring some matches with me? You can see a bit if you get up really close – but not enough.

Footsteps! Hazel and I whip round – but it's an old man shuffling along with his dog. He certainly doesn't look like a hardened criminal. He's puffing on one of those ultra pungent French cigarettes. Aha.

"Hang on, Hazel," I say – and I bound across the road and accost him.

"Excusez-moi, Monsieur," I start eagerly.

He cowers away from me and calls sharply to his dog. Oh gosh, he thinks I'm going to mug him!

"Non! Non! Je suis une amie," I gabble hastily.

He looks at me as if I'm quite mad. His dog bares its teeth. I finally convince him that I only want a match. He tuts at me, but he fumbles in his pocket and produces a matchbox. I hope he'll give me the box. Or a handful of matches. But he gives me just one measly little match.

I thank him all the same and he shuffles on.

"You shouldn't talk to strange men," says Hazel.

"He seemed to think I was a strange girl," I say. "Now. Where's the most likely place for this sign? On the corner, I suppose. Let's look there."

109

We go to the corner building and look at it carefully. I feel with my fingers but there doesn't seem to be any carved lettering anywhere.

"Maybe it's higher up," I say. "Hazel? Can you lift me up onto your shoulders?"

Hazel looks appalled.

"Oh come on. Look, it's easy. Bend down, and I'll sort of sit on your shoulders, and then you straighten up. Come on, I'm not very heavy."

Hazel groans and staggers and sighs as if she's hoisting Billy Bunter aloft. We both nearly go flying – but she manages to steady herself at last, so I can have a feel along the wall.

"No. Move along a bit. No, not that far. There!" I nudge her gently with my foot.

"Don't you dare kick me!"

"I wasn't kicking! But I think I've found it. There's all scratchy lettering on this bit."

I strike the match on the wall – and there, gloriously illuminated, in slightly shaky lettering, is *Rue des Rats*.

"Hurray, hurray, it *is*," I say, bouncing about in my enthusiasm.

Which means in effect that I'm bouncing on Hazel, and she doesn't appreciate this. I slide down off her shoulders and give them a cursory massage while she winces and wails.

"No more time for physiotherapy. We've got to find our hiding place." I look across the street. "There's a hotel there – with a little garden."

Hazel sees where I'm looking.

"Stevie! We can't go in there. It's trespassing."

"We're just going in the garden, that's all. And if anyone catches us we'll just say we wanted to look at the flowers. They can't possibly object to that. Come on." I take her hand and pull her inside. "There! Now, we can still see the corner building where the sign is. We just

110

wait here – and then when the meeting actually takes place we take the photo." A sudden terrible thought occurs to me. "Hazel? Has your camera got a flash?"

"Oh yes. You just press a button and it activates it. Nan showed me."

"Hurrah for your Nan," I say. "What's the time? Nearly half past eleven. Not long to wait now!"

And yet it certainly seems a long wait. A very very long wait indeed. We can't really risk talking too much in case someone hears us. We just lurk in the dark garden – and every now and then I peer at my watch.

We keep on waiting. And waiting. And waiting and waiting.

My friend Cathy told me that it can be terribly boring keeping watch for someone. She sometimes has to do it hour after hour. She says it isn't half a strain on one's patience – and one's bladder too. Hazel seems to have this problem. She's shifting uncomfortably from foot to foot.

"Stevie, I'm dying to – " she whispers.

"You can't," I whisper back.

Hazel sniffs miserably.

"You've got the camera all set and ready?"

"Yes."

"And the flash?"

"*Yes!*"

"Sh!"

"Well honestly," whispers Hazel. "I'll take the wretched photo, I promise. I won't let you down. *If* they turn up. You do realize, don't you, Stevie, that we're crouching in a garden in the middle of Paris at nearly midnight just because of one of your famous bizarre hunches. You're so sure you're right, but honestly, it's not very likely, is it?"

"Shut up, Haze."

"No, I won't shut up. Think about that poor student

111

on the boat. You were absolutely convinced he was a murderer. You were completely up the creek there, weren't you? And I bet you are this time too. I bet we've taken all these risks and we're going to get into tremendous trouble when we finally get back, all for *nothing* –"

"Shut *up*!" I hiss, and I put my hand over Hazel's mouth. Because I can hear footsteps. Light tapping footsteps. I can tell Hazel hears them too, because she stops struggling and freezes.

I bob up so I can have a proper look. It's Mr Smoothie's girlfriend! It *is*! She's carrying a briefcase, clutching it close to her chest. She's wearing a headscarf and a trenchcoat and high heels that click as she walks. The clicks aren't very even. She's so nervous that her legs must be shaking.

Her footsteps get slower and slower as she approaches the corner building. I crouch down again, not wanting to risk her spotting me, though it's so dark it doesn't seem likely. Her footsteps carry on for a moment or two and I screw my face up, terrified that she's going to go on walking, that it's all a false alarm, she's probably not Mr Smoothie's girl at all but some perfectly ordinary innocent woman out for a walk.

But the footsteps stop! I wait. Then very very cautiously I bob up. She's waiting there on the corner, right underneath the sign. I peer at my watch in the dark. Only a couple of minutes to go.

I can hear Hazel breathing sharp panicky little breaths. I point to the camera and she lifts it up in the air, getting ready.

We wait. The girl over the road waits. She keeps looking at her watch. Then she looks up the road, down the road. I can't see her face at all but her whole *body* looks tense.

We go on waiting. I have a terrible tickle start up in my

throat and swallow like mad, terrified I might start coughing. Even my swallowing sounds like a roar to my own ears. And then I hear a distant church chiming. It's midnight.

The girl pointlessly gives her watch another check. We wait. Oh no, something's *got* to happen now. It'll just be too awful if the three of us wait on and on and on all night long, and nobody comes.

But then I suddenly hear the distant hum of a car engine. It's getting nearer. The girl's figure straightens. She's heard it too. I give Hazel a little nudge to get her ready.

The car's getting nearer still, actually in the street. The girl holds up her briefcase in readiness. She must have the money inside. The car's slowing down. I can't see who's driving it. It could be Mr Scruffy, but it's so difficult to tell in this light.

Hazel's standing up too, camera poised. We're all ready!

But it happens so quickly I can hardly take it in. I thought the car would stop, they'd talk, examine the contents of the briefcase, the proffered package. But there's hardly any interaction at all. The car doesn't even stop properly. It just slows beside the girl, the window nearest her open. She steps forward, hands in the briefcase and receives a smallish package.

"Quick!" I hiss at Hazel.

She takes the photograph, the flash brilliant in the dark, almost blinding me. And the girl. She stares over at us, gasping, obviously panicking.

"Oh no. She's seen us," I say.

They've seen us in the car too – but they don't stop to find out who we are. The engine revs and they speed off – and I don't even get time to take in their number plate because the girl's running over to us, desperate.

"Stevie! What are we going to do?" Hazel screams.

113

"She's going to get us."

"There are two of us against one of her," I hiss – but she's got her hand in her pocket and oh God, what's that, is it a gun? No, it's a knife, a small but deadly knife, its blade glinting in the darkness.

She's pointing it right at Hazel.

"Give me that camera, you stupid little girl," she shouts.

Hazel stares at her, stares at the knife, unable to move.

We *can't* let her have the camera. We'll have gone through all this for nothing.

I suddenly snatch the camera from Hazel's hands and run for it.

"Stevie! Oh Stevie, be careful!" Hazel screams. "Watch out! She's coming after you."

I can run fast, but she's running too, she's kicked off her high heels and is pounding after me in her bare feet, and when I glance over my shoulder I see that awful knife. I run blindly forwards, make the corner, and then smash straight into a lamp post. I reel round dizzily, waiting for the thump in my back as the knife goes in.

But there's no thump, no sharp pain, no gush of blood. There's a scream, but it's not mine. It's the girl's! Because just as she's coming for me, knife raised, yelling for the camera, Hazel gets to her, Hazel flings herself forward, Hazel grabs her round the kneecaps in an amazing rugby tackle, Hazel sends her flying. *Hazel*!

"Don't you *dare* stab Stevie!" Hazel shrieks, tumbling on top of her.

The girl's still got the knife but before she can twist round and use it I stop reeling. I snap into serious action, and grab her hard round the wrist, jerking it so that she groans and has to let the knife go. I grab it myself and then sit right down on her head.

"There! We've got her! Oh Hazel, well done, well

done! That's it, keep sitting on her. You were brilliant, do you know that? I didn't know you could run so fast. And the way you tackled her! They'll have you playing Rugby for England if you don't watch out!"

"Oh Stevie," says Hazel happily. "*I* didn't know I could either. It was just when I saw her with that knife I just sort of *shot* forward because I knew I had to stop her."

The girl squirms and groans beneath us.

"You shut up and keep still," Hazel says gruffly, new menace in her voice. Then she looks at me. "What do we do now, Stevie? I mean, we can't keep sitting on her all night, can we?"

"We scream for help," I say.

"But what if Mr Smoothie comes – or the men in the car?"

"They've all cleared off and left her to it," I say. "Come on, Haze, Scream."

We scream and scream.

"Help! Au secours! Nous sommes sitting sur une méchante voleur – voleuse? Gendarmes! Call a gendarme, beaucoup de gendarmes tout de suite!" I bellow with what I think is great presence of mind and linguistic ability.

They say at home in England you can shout your head off for help and nobody comes because they're so scared of getting involved. But thank goodness it doesn't seem to be like that in France. People come hurtling in all directions. They explode with frantic questions, none of which I can understand. One stupid woman keeps trying to haul me off the girl's head, but if I'm crazy enough to get up she'll get away.

"Non, non, you sit on her aussi. Elle est méchante," I insist. "Pas moi! Je suis une detective. Gendarme! Get the gendarmes. Telephonez, s'il vous plaît."

Thank goodness someone's telephoned, because

before long a police van draws up and various assorted gendarmes hurtle out.

There's more questions, and this time Hazel and I have to get up off the girl. She staggers to her feet and starts a torrent of fluent French – I think she's saying she was just walking by when *we* attacked her! And the gendarmes are listening to her, looking as if they might actually believe her. She looks so ultra ordinary and respectable – whereas Haze and I look like a couple of those gypsy girls. But *she's* the criminal!

"Look for her packet!" I cry. "Dans her mackintosh. Les hommes dans l'auto gave it to her. Regardez dans her pocket!"

She turns out her pockets – and there's nothing there! Oh no, did she throw the packet away somewhere when she started to chase after me? But she'd never do that, not when the contents must be worth a fortune.

So where else could she hide it?

"Down her chest!" I yell.

I don't know the French for it, but I point – and then suddenly snatch at her mackintosh front. The gendarme nearest me tries to catch my wrist, but I'm too quick for him. I reach right inside her mac – and there's the package!

The girl shouts at me furiously as I hold it aloft. The gendarme takes it from me, opens the brown paper, and then unscrews the plastic packaging inside. There's just silvery white powder there, looking like castor sugar.

But the policemen whistle and they murmur one word. Cocaine!

So they arrest her and then although they don't speak much English and I suppose we don't really speak much French they congratulate Hazel and me and ask us to tell them how exactly we're involved in all this. I launch into a long elaborate story, embroidering a little, while everyone around me marvels.

But then we're all driven off in the police van to the station and Hazel and I are separately interviewed by some high up French policeman who speaks perfect English – and I have to go through it all over again, this time a strictly accurate unadulterated version.

I give him as good a description of Mr Smoothie and Mr Scruffy as I possibly can.

"But surely the girl will tell you who they are and where to find them?" I say. "After all, they set her up and then deserted her."

"The girl is in love," says the policeman, raising his eyebrows expressively. "How do you say it in English? Her lips are stuck up."

"Sealed, actually. But it means the same. What an absolute idiot!"

I know she threatened us with the knife, but I'm not certain she'd actually have used it. She's not the real criminal who set it all up – Mr Smoothie is."

"I can't bear it if he goes free! Still, maybe there's a chance of getting the men in the car. My friend took a flash photo of them, it's real evidence."

I proffer the camera proudly. The policeman looks at it eagerly. He examines it. Then he looks at me quizzically.

"Your friend, Mademoiselle? Is this the first photograph she has taken with this film?"

"Oh no. She's taken lots of snaps. The film must be nearly finished by now."

"I'm afraid not. You see this little number here? Number one. I think your friend has been forgetting to wind the film on each time she takes the photograph. She has taken many photographs, yes – but all on top of each other!"

I give a little scream of despair – but I can't really be cross with Hazel, even though we haven't got our evidence after all. And in actual fact we don't need it, because before we leave the station the French police tell us that the men in the car were stopped for speeding on the outskirts of Paris. They acted so suspiciously that the officers investigated and found the briefcase stuffed with money. So now they're under arrest too – and let's hope they'll split on Mr Smoothie so he can be put safely behind bars. He's the real rat.

The police drive Hazel and me back to our hotel in a very stylish limousine. We feel very proud of ourselves – only it's a pity it's now four o'clock in the morning and there's no one to see us.

They have to ring at the hotel doorway for quite a long time. Then there are dealings with the night porter and Madame – and then Mrs Wainwright comes rushing downstairs, with her hair in *curlers* and an amazing shocking pink nylon nightie adorning her ample curves. When she sees the police and Hazel and me she goes white and starts whimpering.

She can't quite take it in when the police start congratulating her for being the teacher of such extraordinary quick-thinking young heroines. Heroines, that's the very word!

It's not the word Mrs Wainwright uses when she gets us on our own. She is so furiously angry with us that she goes as pink as her nightie – but then she suddenly bursts into tears and says "Still, thank God you're both all right, you terrible pair," and she holds out her arms and *hugs* us. There we are, cuddled close to the capacious bosom. Haze and I are so stunned by the experience we roll our eyes at each other, positively *boggling*.

And everyone else boggles at breakfast next morning when they hear about us and all our amazing nocturnal exploits. We tell the story over and over again. Even Mr Mason and Ms Mosely listen all agog.

"I feel awful that I didn't believe you before, Stevie," says Mr Mason. "And I even called you a liar. So you can

118

call me a complete wally, if you like."

"And me," says Ms Mosely.

I chuckle at such a delightful invitation.

"And I can't get over how brave you were too, Hazel," says Mr Mason. "Stevie says you saved her life with this incredible rugby tackle."

"Well – it was more a trip than a tackle," says Hazel, determinedly honest.

"I think you were marvellous anyway," says Mr Mason.

Hazel is practically swooning by this time.

"Hazel certainly isn't a drip, is she?" I say, looking meaningfully at Ms Mosely.

"Why didn't you tell *me* what was going on?" Terry asks, taking me on one side. "You could have got me and my mates to help you out."

"Well Terry, you were actually otherwise engaged," I say sweetly, glancing at the angora rabbit.

"I think you've got the wrong idea about Lucy and me," says Terry. "I suppose she's sort of my girlfriend now. Well, *she* says she is. But she'll never *ever* be a real mate like you."

I think I'm flattered. I rather like the idea of being Terry's real mate. But I know who my real best ever mate is. Good old Hazel. She might be a bit thick where cameras are concerned and she might have a hang-up about heights – but so what? She's the bravest friend in all the world.

I start acting out her famous rugby tackle again and they all start cheering. They're cheering me too, of course. Well, I don't blame them really.

The Pit
Ann Cheetham

The summer has hardly begun when Oliver Wright is plunged into a terrifying darkness. Gripped by fear when workman Ted Hoskins is reduced to a quivering child at a demolition site, Oliver believes something of immense power has been disturbed. But what?

Caught between two worlds – the confused present and the tragic past – Oliver is forced to let events take over.

An Armada Original

The Witch of Lagg

Neither Colin, Oliver nor Prill is looking forward to
spending their holidays with gloomy Grierson of
Lagg's Castle. They nickname the creepy mansion
'Castle Dracula' but the terrible secret it hides is more
sinister and more complicated than that of a vampire.
As the cousins explore the icy rooms and the dark
woods, they find themselves victims of an ancient, evil
and murderous force . . .

Other spinechilling novels by Ann Cheetham include:

Black Harvest
The Beggar's Curse
The Pit

Armada

MacGyver on Ice
Mark Daniel

In the Alaskan wastelands, a crazy general has developed a bacterial time-bomb which threatens to wipe out the neighbouring Russian population. Only one man can break through Abe Roscow's ingenious security defences and abort his deadly plan – MacGyver, ex-Special Services officer, a fast-thinking loner who combines a brilliant mind with formidable physical strength.

An Armada Original

On the Spot
Mark Daniel

Ben O'Connell has a problem. He is small. Humiliated at home and bullied at school, he seems a born loser. But Ben has a special talent for snooker and he's determined to reach the top.

It seems that no one can beat him and nothing will stand in his way – until scheming Perry Curling becomes his manager. To him, a boy like Ben is made for hustling round seedy snooker joints. Winning championships, says Curling, is the stuff dreams are made of. After all, this is tough '80s Merseyside.

But Ben is aiming for the top . . .

An Armada Original

The Messenger
Monica Dickens

What is wrong with the house next door? When Rose's parents buy it, to turn into an annexe for the Wood Briar Hotel, they brighten it with cheerful colours and pretty patterns. But the house has a terrible effect on people, filling them with a sense of tragedy and despair. What is the secret of the deep, dark cupboard with its strange smell of the sea? What horror from the past casts its shadow upon the living?

When Rose becomes thirteen – 'that special age' as the surprising Mr Vingo puts it, 'when your mind and spirit are aroused to a state of tempestuous movement' – she is chosen to be a messenger of the Great Grey Horse.

Noble, beautiful and brave, the horse was long ago the favourite charger of the vile Lord of the Moor, and his heroism in the face of treachery saved a whole village. Now he lives on, with a mission to protect innocent people from evil, misery and violence.

A tune played on Mr Vingo's marmalade-coloured piano summons Rose to the horse, and she is galloped back through time into the heart of the mystery. Can she meet the horse's challenge? Can she find a way to break the spell of tragedy? As the horse's messenger she must not fail . . .

This is the first book about Rose and the Great Grey Horse. There are three further titles available in Armada: *Ballad of Favour*, *The Haunting of Bellamy 4* and *Cry of a Seagull*.

Ballad of Favour
Monica Dickens

A small child's cry of fear is the beginning of a new adventure for Rose Wood, chosen messenger of Favour, the magical Great Grey Horse.

What does it mean? Rose knows that when the horse carries her into different scenes and different times, she is supposed to find clues there.

'The child might have been abandoned – it might have been hurt,' she tells her friend Mr Vingo. 'But I don't know who it was or where it was or when it was.'

'Trust the horse,' says Mr Vingo. 'He'll show you.'

Centuries ago the horse belonged to the repulsive Lord of the Moor, and found fame in his heroic race to save a village. Now he lives on to fight against evil and despair.

As his messenger, Rose must fly with him to a small, decrepit, back street, and learn what makes the child cry so pitifully. The clues are there – a railway line, a fun fair, a TV programme, a birthday – but how do they fit together? Rose must find the solution before it is too late.

This is the sequel to Monica Dickens' first book about Rose and the Great Grey Horse, *The Messenger*. There are a further two titles available in Armada: *The Haunting of Bellamy 4* and *Cry of a Seagull*.

Armada

Famous Stories
available in Armada include

Armada

Have you seen
NANCY DREW
lately?

Nancy Drew has become a girl of the 80s! There is hardly a girl from seven to seventeen who doesn't know her name.

Now you can continue to enjoy Nancy Drew in a new series, written for older readers – THE NANCY DREW FILES. Each book has more romance, fashion, mystery and adventure.

In THE NANCY DREW FILES, Nancy pursues one thrilling adventure after another. With her boundless energy and intelligence, Nancy finds herself enrolling at a crime-ridden high school, attending rock concerts and locating the missing star, skiing in Vermont with friends Bess and George and faithful boyfriend Ned, and temping at a teenage magazine based in wildly exciting New York.

COMING IN SPRING 1988

The Nancy Drew Files

    No. 1 Secrets Can Kill
    No. 2 Deadly Intent
    No. 3 Murder on Ice
    No. 4 Smile and Say Murder

ARMADA

Forthcoming teenage fiction
published in Armada

Class of 88 1–4
Linda A. Cooney

In A Spin
Mark Daniel

Nightmare Park
Linda Hoy

Sin Bin 1–4
Keith Miles

Run With the Hare
Linda Newbery

ARMADA